DREAMS WITHIN DREAMS

Serial One: Omnipresence

Copyright 2023 © M.D. Boncher

1st Edition

Cover Design: M. D. Boncher

LINKS & SOCIAL MEDIA

If you enjoyed the book, the best thing you can do for an indie author like myself is leave a review from where you purchased the book and any other social media outlets you enjoy. Let others know what you think, including the author. Your reviews are appreciated.

For news on all creative projects of M.D. Boncher, you can find updates, communication and news at:

www.thedreamnebula.com

or at my Guilded channel at

Resonant Point

www.guilded.gg/i/Eoe4QVVk

BIBLIOGRAPHY

Wild Adventure Sci-Fi

Tales From the Dream Nebula

01. Dreams Within Dreams

02. Lucid Reality

03. The Living Nightmares

Dark Christian Fantasy

Akiniwazisaga

A Light Rises in a Dark World

The Inheritance Thieves

Into The High Places

TABLE OF CONTENTS

TALES from the
DREAM NEBULA
01

1..

Winston stared at the black and white flickers of an ancient film on the television and took another long sip from his glass. Heavy ice cubes clanked in the thick cut crystal tumbler. He shifted back and forth to get comfortable on his living room couch. With a sigh, he traced his thumb along the raised diamond pattern of his glass, and lost himself in the fiction playing out before him.

On screen, a detective caught the dirty little stool pigeon in another lie and gave him the third degree by means of a sharp sock to the jaw. The mousy little bug-eyed man whined and groaned as he spilled his guts. A smile wanted to touch Winston's lips, but apathy tamped it back down. Mesmerized by the ancient entertainment from a planet and culture which no longer existed, his mind drifted.

Humanity's home was gone. Conquered by a malevolent cosmic force that carved up the

Earth and Sun and swallowed it. Adding the remains to its incomprehensible form. Earth's survivors lived on the interstellar wreckage of the entire Sol system clinging to their cultural artifacts with bitter nostalgia. Now all humanity lived in the Dream, subject to its eternal master.

"Winston?" a woman's voice called from somewhere behind him. He frowned and made an effort to ignore it. Emmy, his daughter, continued to play her quiet game on the living room carpet, pushing her dolls around in toy cars, making up her own stories.

"Winston!" the woman's voice was sharper, his frown deepened. Where was that voice coming from? Was she even in the house? It didn't sound like she was outside.

"Hun, I think Mother is here," his wife's voice drifted in from the kitchen. Valerie was making lunch. Winston smiled at the clanking of dishes and the whiff of barbecue ham sandwiches.

There was a terrific pounding at the door as Mother battered it with her fist.

"Winstaah-ahahahahssssss-on-on-nnnn-stonn!" Mother's voice stuttered and chipmunked from data packet loss as his anti-virus programs fought to keep her out. She must be trying to hack his home instance, and her connection had lagged out for a moment.

He sighed as she overwhelmed his local server's security- again. A curse for all AIs rattled around his head.

"Go away, Mother!" he shouted over his shoulder, taking his eyes off the movie. He could hear Valerie leave the kitchen, walking quickly to open the front door.

"Val! Don't let her in. I don't want to deal with her cheis right now," he swore. "There's a reason I locked the instance."

"Okay, Hun," Val replied and went back to her cooking, humming a Stepfordesque tune. Emmy ignored the racket while Winston turned up the movie's sound.

"Oh for the love of..." came a growl from Mother. With a terrific splintering bang, she forced her way through the locked front door in a spray of pixels and static that rippled throughout the home.

Mother looked like a woman in her forties or fifties, dressed in a sharp dove gray suit, jacket with big shoulders, an A-Line skirt, and a bright white blouse with a string of black pearls with a copper and emerald broach on her left lapel. She looked like she had stepped out of the movie Winston was watching. Mother strutted into the living room on impressive heels. Her blond-turning-white hair was in a tight bun, with two strands framing her perturbed expression.

"Nahq it!" Winston hollered spilling his Brandy Old-Fashioned. He shot up off his couch and glared at her angrily. "Can't you take the hint?"

"Nahq it yourself! Billy Joe Bob and I have been pinging you for three hours. You know better than to log out when you're being unloaded! I'm hardly surprised to find you here in your own little Levitown shrine watching old movies."

"In costume today, Mother?" Winston stifled a snort of mockery at his freight broker's appearance.

She sneered at his comment. "No. Your behnging server blended my avatar code in with your stupid movie," she snapped.

"And so what if I've been down for three hours on the dock? Those lumpers normally take my whole ten hour break to get me unloaded. I've probably got another five hours left!" Winston snapped back.

"This was a hot load, Winston! They started offloading you the instant you bumped their dock. They've been done for hours, and have been screaming at me to get you moved! There are a lot of other loads waiting to get in here. Need I remind you, I do not take kindly to being screamed at by an overclocked wirey warehouse manager every five minutes while you play 'Father Knows Bankruptcy' in this... this..." she waved her hands around at Winston's simulation, "Americana nightmare! And bankruptcy, I might add, is precisely what you're facing if you get kicked off this account!"

Val came into the living room, wiping her hands on her apron that screamed Pre-Dream American Golden Age ruffles.

"Hun, would you like me to escort Mother out?" her pleasant voice held a hint of iron as server security warnings leaked into her voice.

"Try it and I'll turn you into a thermostat subroutine, missy!" Mother snapped with a sharp taloned finger thrust at Valerie.

"Nahq it! All of you, shut up!" Winston shouted. "Fine, mother, I'll get off the dock and get rolling."

"That's all I ever wanted," Mother sighed and gave a patronizing smile.

He opened up the route planner app for his tug, the Sierra Madre. The 'pending' load interface was blank.

"Wait. They show I'm unloaded, but there's no backhaul?" Winston asked. "I always get a backhaul."

"Since you didn't clear the dock right away, their loadmaster chose to go with a different vendor," Mother said, arms crossed.

"Come on! For sleeping three hours on his dock?" Winston whined.

"This isn't the first time you've pulled this stunt with them," Mother reminded him. "You were warned there'd be consequences. Once you're rolling, contact the guardpost on the way out for further instructions."

"And what the Purg does that mean?" Winston shouted.

"They wouldn't tell me. Said they'd only talk to you."

"Of all the bullcheis powertrips," Winston ranted. "You're my freight broker. You book my jobs. Get me a backhaul home!"

"I'll see what I can do, but don't expect much. Also, lose the attitude. Your self inflicted wounds do not grant you the right to make me your emotional punching bag," Mother fussed and then vanished in a cascade of pixels falling to the living room carpet.

He stared stupidly at the pile she deliberately inserted into his simulation. The mess was an icon of rebuke and criticism of his actions and manner toward her. She could be petty like that.

Winston let out a growl that escalated into a frustrated scream as he ended his connection and exited from his home instance.

2.

Winston's consciousness slammed back into his body with a myoclonic jerk. It felt like he was dropped ten feet into his bed. He jerked off the induction rig headband, threw it back onto his pillow and gave a tired groan. The memory of his argument with Mother came forward as he rubbed his eyes.

There was a gentle knock at the door. Billy Joe Bob must have heard him wake up.

"Hoss, y'all gonna get up in there?" came the autotuned voice of his loadmaster.

Winston said nothing and swung his legs over the side. The Sierra Madre's sleeper was roomy as tug accommodations went. Just big enough for a generous bunk, a small bathroom, kitchenette with ample overhead cabinets and storage lockers under the mattress. His rumpled flight suit felt grimy with sweat. No time to clean up he thought, looking at the cramped shower. It was time to get rolling. Grabbing a battered cap, he got up and opened the sleeper door.

Billy Joe Bob glided back out of Winston's way as he shuffled into the cockpit.

"Mother's all sorts of mad, and that dock boss has been bangin' on the canopy off and on for an hour. Paint's busted up on the side of the sleeper but nothin' that cain't be taken care of." The industrial mechoid prattled on, like a dutiful but rather clueless deputy.

Billy Joe Bob's face was warm and friendly, covered with a flexible skin of smartex. A sophisticated rubber that could mimic muscles almost perfectly, save for being rather glossy and in Billy Joe's case, light gray. Biological beings were usually freaked out by an incomprehensible sensor suite for a head, even insectoid features disturbed most sentient species. His human-like chest was covered in a polished chromed alloy perched on top of a rotund "beer-belly" bulge under which sat an upside-down dish shaped like a wok at his beltline. This covered the top of a pile of nanomachines that looked like glittering black volcanic sand which reminded Winston of an ankle length maxi-skirt or a samurai kimono.

The mechoid's arms were brawny caricatures made of the same nanosand as his lower body. They stuck to shallow dishes at his shoulders. It seemed like an incongruous mix of metal, rubber and grit but it worked as a whole. Just another hard-workin' good ol' mech.

The ship canopy's particle shield was closed keeping the cab dark. The only light came from holomonitors and blinking LEDs of the Sierra Madre's controls. An angry red pulse from the comm suite indicated Mother was on the line. The large number of missed messages snarled at him in a red insistent font from her and Omnifeed.

So what if he slept on the dock, what was the big deal? These facilities were always in a 'hurry up and wait' mindset. Why all the urgency?

Winston grunted at Billy Joe as he took the few steps to the trio of bridge seats in the middle of the cab. The co-pilot and navigator's seats had been empty so long they had a light layer of dust on the cushions. Winston refused to fill them after he bought the Sierra Madre. Those jobs were farmed out to non-sentient AIs. It was just him and Billy Joe out here and he wanted it to remain that way. Even Billy Joe didn't pretend to have those human characteristics. He just hung in his service rack for downtime or stood out of the way, secured to the deck by his skirt.

Flopping into the pilot's seat, Winston pulled the crash frame down, and wrapped himself securely in place. He started a quick instrument pre-trip checklist. A smooth rumble grew as the grav fans deepened their vortexes. Their atmospheric draw transferred a subtle vibration to the Sierra Madre's cab.

Green gauges across the board.

The monitors on the pair of bulk trailers he was hitched to woke up and reported back their tractor beams were double hooked and working properly. A quick check of the dock lock showed the Sierra Madre was already free and at station-keeping. All was go for departure.

The message light continued its accusatory glare. With a sigh of resolution, Winston parted the particulate shield. As the thick plates slid back the

Dream came into view in a glorious bright golden glow.

The clouds went on forever in all the colors of the sunset. Darker blots of green, black and brown skylands drifting among them. These chunks of planets and asteroids floated in the endless sky of the Dream like the islands of Earth, before it was torn apart and incorporated into Xiao the Eternal's empire.

Closer in, Omnifeed's huge industrial complex was peppered with other draymen waiting for their dock, or jockeying back and forth to the anchorage point. Some had only one trailer hooked on to their tugs and tractors, others were pulling sky trains with more than ten over-sized containers. A one-thousand trailer train streamed through the sky like a titanic snake. Off in the distance, skyland-sized bulk dirigibles loomed like whales among fish.

The retracting shields plates slowly revealed more of this busy scene. Four open intakes of gravity fans came into view, as the shield plates locked back into their housings. Dull rainbow flickers licked out from their open maws when something more substantial than gas was sucked through their gravity shear planes. When under power, anything that passed through the rings was crushed and mangled by the tidal forces.

Winston threw on the Sierra Madre's running lights and fired up his nav computer's course projector which plotted a hologram path through the chaos in the air in front of his seat.

"Hoss, look out." Billy Joe said and pointed out the window.

A man was flying from a tug parked danger-close to him on his Bumblebee flight harness.

"That jackass," Winston grumbled.

The man landed nimbly on the Sierra Madre's canopy. Looking down between his feet, he began making threatening gestures with a wrench, yelling in a language Winston didn't understand.

"Get the behng off my hull!" Winston shouted and slapped the horn. A low chord of ear shattering sound rattled the air. The irate pilot slapped his hands over his ears and staggered. Winston smiled as the man was no longer interested in cussing at him in his gobbledy tongue. Apparently he decided to tell Winston off without putting on ear protection. One hundred and forty decibels at close range will make sure he never tries that again.

"Shut down number four, Hoss," Billy Joe Bob shouted. The careless pilot had staggered too far back and was about to be dragged through the fan.

Winston's hand was already hitting the emergency shutdown for the number four fan just as the gravity well plucked the careless pilot up and fired him through its maw. The tidal forces, though no longer fatal, shot the man through its open vortex at hundreds of miles per hour, zipping past Winston's trailers like a musketball.

"Uhhh..." drawled Billy Joe Bob in horror, realizing what just happened.

"Way ahead of you, Bubby." Winston said, now wide eyed and fully awake. That pilot's Bumblebee protected him from splattering against something big and hard. At least the man could float back to his tractor, once he regained his senses, Winston consoled himself.

He sounded the tug's horn again signaling his departure from the dock with one long blast followed by a pair of short toots in the traditional signal for departing port. The Sierra Madre eased out of her dock and followed her assigned buoy path toward the guard post.

Winston stared grimly out the canopy. His mind whirling on the repercussions of what had just happened. It was not his fault. That pilot climbed onto his tug without proper gear. Inside a restricted area no less. The fact that Winston saved his life by shutting down the grav fan in time made it all just a near miss. No one was really hurt. Right? Just pride and ego. Cheis, cheis, cheis.

"You think we're in trouble?" Billy Joe asked.

"We'll find out soon enough, Bubby," Winston sighed.

A scrambled call came into his comm suite. Priority one.

Winston tapped the channel open and his comms unscrambled the transmission.

"This is the Sierra Madre, receiving you. Over," He answered as calmly as he could muster.

"Sierra Madre, this is Omnifeed Control," said the professional sounding voice. The guardpost's dataoids had voices modeled after the ancient cadence of flight controller speak. No matter what, everyone was equal in their eyes, or so the timbre of their words implied.

"Go ahead Omnifeed Control. Over." Winston squinted hard, gritting his teeth as he waited for the reply.

"You are charged with violating Omnifeed site safety rules. Furthermore, you violated rules of professional conduct by failing to leave the dock when ordered, and committing acts that may have resulted in injury to another contractor," the guardpost stated.

"Hey, he climbed on my hull! Without safety gear! I shut down the fan in time," Winston complained. "Blame him!"

"Your objections are heard and understood. The pilot will be dealt with accordingly," came the dataoid's reply. Winston could hear the 'but' hanging unsaid. "Regardless, you have four previous violations of loading dock policy in the last five weeks. Your company, Harper Enterprises, a subcontractor for Motherroad Logistics, is hereby suspended from all Omnifeed facilities for six months due to these infractions. After that time you may reapply to be an approved carrier."

"Aw, come on!" Winston shouted at the digital sentient.

"For the safety incident, you are hereby personally permabanned from this specific facility." The passionless words were worse than being cussed at.

"I'm being permabanned for him violating your policy? He climbed on me!" Winston shouted.

"His discipline is a private matter. Be glad if he is unharmed. In case there is permanent injury and medical bills, your legal information has been provided to his agent," Omnifeed Control said without compassion.

"You have no right to do that!" Winston protested, slamming his fist against the armrest.

"That is the law in accordance with Xiao's Imperial covenants and protocols of commerce. Hail, Xiao the Eternal," the dataoid controller added reflexively. "To paraphrase the relative covenant, 'Omnifeed, as a third-party witness, must report what was recorded to maintain good standing with the Empire.' We maintain the highest Imperial commerce rating and will protect it with all due legal effort."

Winston let out a defeated sigh, and as if she could hear it, his comm bleeped again as Mother tried to get through.

"Copy all that Omnifeed Control. Sierra Madre out."

The other comm continued to blink. Numbly, Winston's unfocused eyes stared toward a non-existent horizon.

Was this the start of the final plunge? He flew above the anchorage point toward the perimeter buoys that marked Omnifeed's airspace boundaries, itching to drop the hammer and bolt out of there.

Would he be rockbound and stuck on the Imperial dole because he just couldn't get work after the Sierra Madre was impounded and he was blackballed?

Omnifeed was his last regular client. If Mother could even use him on another job it would be low paying spot work from here on out. Last second frantic runs to cover mistakes for people who dropped the ball and deserved to get burned. Sure, you could look the hero doing that, but the hassle. Oh, my Xiao! The hassle!

Winston flipped the comm from Mother open but said nothing.

"It isn't as bad as you may think, Winston." Mother's words were gentle.

"It certainly isn't good. Did the payment process out?" Winston drummed his fingers against the arms of his seat.

"Yes. We're paid in full, so there's a little money in the kitty, but you can kiss your insurance goodbye. I have several texts to respond to from Omnifeed, and that moron pilot's shyster lawyer."

"Did you see Omnifeed's evidence?" Winston said, his voice rising on a hint of faint hope.

"I did. He was at fault and so I might be able to get a lawyer in to provide a good defense and resolve this while paying out only for some lost time and wages."

"Mother, did I ever tell you that I loved you?" Winston said with a smirk. Behind him Billy Joe Bob let out an arpeggiated laugh.

"Eugh!" Mother let out a strangled retch. "You biomes and your erratic emotions." Winston knew she appreciated his sentiment, otherwise she wouldn't have called him such a dirty name as 'biome'.

"Okay, I know we're on the bubble, so what's next, Mother? Am I untouchable now?" Winston asked, as he adjusted his course from the anchorage.

"I'll put some feelers out and see what I can find," Mother said and hung up before Winston could reply.

At least she hadn't abandoned him, he thought with a sigh. She understood he slept plugged in his home instance to keep the nightmares away. Winston knew he screwed up, but it wasn't like he had been impairing himself on the job.

The Sierra Madre slowly passed a giant dirigible bulk hauler. Her gravity planes were shifted sideways toward Omnifeed's digesters where they made SiCHON feedstock for nanofabricators all across the Dream. Pipes and silos filled Winston's view in a chaotic flurry as they flew down the flight corridor towards the outer marker. Then in a flash, they exited the complex into open sky.

Winston flipped through his cameras to watch the Omnifeed facility recede behind him, and turned toward home on Pseudomaha. He glared at the big nanofabrication silos with the giant Omnifeed logo on their side. The facility disappeared behind a cloying yellow cloud of sulfur dust.

"Hoss, you want me doin' anything right now?" Billy Joe Bob asked.

"You got chores left?" Winston's eyes remained focused on the traffic sensors. The little blobs of blue, green, yellow and red, slid past with neon trails in the holographic hud.

"Naw. Not really. Containers are empty and undamaged. We have an extra free day rental with 'em before getting them back to Consolidated Freight for maintenance." Billy Joe said.

"Rog that," Winston said. "I got nothing for you then. Hit the rack and enjoy yourself. We should still have access to Omnifeed's network for another hour or two of flight time. Might as well mooch while we still can. Otherwise, we're 'go-slow' until Mother gets back to me. Maybe we will need that extra free day of rental to get home after all."

"Rog that, Hoss." Billy Joe went to his rack in the back of the cab with a slithering hiss of his nanosand skirt and powered down leaving Winston alone with his worries.

3.

Winston awoke in the pilot's seat with a start by the second chime of the comm. He let out a deep sigh of relief, grateful he had not dreamed. The Sierra Madre was enveloped by a dense smog of who knew what when Mother's call woke him up. All around them were sickly billows of dark green condensates and mini asteroids the size of boulders drifted by. Lightning flickered in the distance off his starboard keel.

Rubbing his gunky face and stubbly chin, Winston started running a position check. Auto pilot did its job. This was just some rogue cloud blowing in from out of the cold outer deeps of the Dream. Thankfully, it wasn't methane. TrafficNet all but ignored it as nothing more than a decorative nuisance, but there was a respiratory advisory out for New Svalbard, Ertoria and Red Provo Station. The Sierra Madre was cruising along at a leisurely mach six and should be in

Pseudomaha in 36 hours at this speed. Plenty of time.

"What's the text, Mother?" Winston said opening the comm link. He'd been asleep for five hours. There was enough interference to the signal from the cloud that his words were being dubbed with subtitles and the lag was around five seconds.

"Well!" Mother exclaimed, "Looks like you got some real sleep. Good for you."

"Thank you. So we've got something?" Winston said and squinted at the 'good boy' tone then nibbled aggressively at a thumbnail, his heel bouncing.

"It's sort of a 'Good, Bad and Ugly' job," Mother said slowly.

"All right." Winston said reservedly, spitting a crescent of fingernail out. "I've never had that choice from you before."

"I've seen these kinds of jobs pop up from time to time, but usually they don't go into a posting like this. Most times it's kept for trusted carriers, which means someone dropped the ball and this is a last minute 'gotta-get-there-now-hurry-hurry' sort of thing, but nobody is available. You just happen to be the best option I can find for them. Assuming you take it."

Winston was grateful for the text captioning. Her voice quality was terrible, nor could he believe his ears.

"Let's go in order. What's the good?" Winston coaxed.

"The job pays well. Very well. Did I say it paid well? Well, it does."

Winston chuckled at her humor.

"How 'well' is 'well'?"

"Low seven figures," Mother said, letting the scale of the payday sink in.

Winston's jaw dropped with a choked gasp.

"Was that you having a stroke?" Mother looked genuinely unsure.

"I think so, Mother," Winston stammered. His mouth flopping and closing like a fish on the shore. "You said low sevens?"

"I did. But it's a take it now or lose it. The contracting broker is on the other comm waiting to book you." Mother's voice was tight, like the pressure was getting to her too.

Winston's other foot started bouncing and he was developing cottonmouth. Seven figures! Even low seven figures was a new start. That kind of money didn't happen unless there was something... dodgy... with it.

"Rog that," he breathed, as if speaking would make this chance vanish. "Is that all the good?"

"Well, container rental is taken care of, you can pick them up at Consolidated when you drop the two on your back now."

Winston was still smiling at the payday."That does make it easy, and you know how I like easy," he let out a sigh, steadying himself. "Okay. What's the bad?"

"It's off the network, so to speak," Mother spoke quickly.

"Wait, I thought you said it was on the job boards?"

"It was," she wheedled, "Just not the job boards I normally use. You're not my only driver you know."

"Just your favorite." Winston said in a mushy voice.

In the silence that followed he could picture her glaring at him.

"Now is not the time to rub that in, Winston Alexander Harper." she threatened. He could practically feel her finger poking him sharply through the speaker.

"Yes Mother," he chuckled. "So this is probably illegal on some point. Who is it not legal with? National, corporate, tribal or Imperial governments?"

"All," came her crackling answer in sync with a sheet of lightning.

Winston blanched and his humor drained out like spilled milk. The single word told him everything he needed to know. Mother had deep connections and friends. He'd always suspected she knew her way around a crooked path better than she ought, but this proved it. Not that she ever brought him near it until now, but he'd never been in such dire straits before. Twelve hours ago, he'd never have been tempted. The last job bought him only a few weeks distance from financial ruin. This was setting him up for a decade. Maybe even for life if he played his cards right.

"What's the ugly, Mother?"

The comm bleeped again as the contract came up. He flipped it open. The shipper and consignee's names were blank and the delivery point was some hot-house moon high in the Dream's upper bands. He was going to sweat his ding-ding off. The list of the ten pre-selected containers were all high armor and hazmat.

"The client won't say, but I have a guess it's not care packages of toys for the good little boys and girls of the Salamandia Contested Zone," Mother said.

Winston had heard of that place. A few princes of Xiao Courts were fighting over who really had control over those skylands and moons. It was a no-go zone for most shippers by corporate decree, not imperial law. No hauler wanted their assets shot up or hijacked. Emperor Xiao seemed more entertained by the fighting than interested in solving the dispute.

"I'm not Santa Claus and this ain't Christmas." Winston said through his fingers. He took his hand from his mouth, trying to let go of the worry that had climbed up on his back. He struggled with all sorts of horrible speculations on what kind of death awaited him if he took it. "A delivery in a war zone. Just perfect."

"If you say no, I understand. Normally I wouldn't send anything there either." There was a pause as she threw him on hold for a moment. "That was the broker. In or out. You have 30 seconds then he's going to take another call and book it with them." Mother said.

"Is there other work?" Winston said.

"I'll book something for you."

Winston knew that meant 'no'.

"Whatever you find is going to be garbage tier, low-pay nonsense that will be barely able to keep up the maintenance on this tug, right?" Winston moaned.

Mother didn't answer.

"Right?" He pushed.

"Ten seconds." Mother deflected.

Winston saw it clearly now. He was blackballed. The instant that idiot flew through his grav fan, no other factor or insurer would touch him. Mother would try to get him work, but even she had her hands tied. The next payment on the Sierra Madre was due in a couple weeks, and then he'd have to shut her down in some vacant lot somewhere because he couldn't dock anywhere. Two months later she'd be repossessed for non-payment on her liens, if she wasn't stripped or stolen by scavengers.

"Seven. He's not playing, Winston. I'm on a clock here. Three," Mother urged.

"Nahq it all! Take it!" Winston burst out. There was no other choice.

Winston hated hearing the words coming out of his mouth the instant he uttered them. "I'll take the behnging job!"

"Done," Mother snapped and was gone, leaving him in silence, with only the dim sound of his engine and the thrum of far off thunder.

4..

Flight time to Consolidated was another eight hours so Winston racked out for real, risking the dreams. As expected they came for him, and they were angry. After being suppressed for so long by his simulated domestic tranquility it was as if they wanted revenge.

~~~

The new smell of the yet unnamed tug was still strong even after a month of piloting her. Jeph, his assigned loadmaster was sitting in the co-pilot's seat, monitoring their return approach to Lougahasa, their home terminal. He was watching a holo-projection was of a local sports feed pre-game analysis show, catching him up on team line-up changes and injury reports for tonight's game.

"Relax, Chingu. We're running on time here. You'll make it to the stadium," Winston said with a chuckle.
~~~

"Chingu yourself," Jeph snipped around a mouthful of Crisptaders, getting crumbs all over the seat. "If I don't make it, it's your money I'm taking for my tickets." His loadmaster then opened up a fantasy sport site and started making some changes to his lineup for the game after one of the talking heads gave new details on a player and how that could affect one of his players.

Winston just smiled with an eye roll. The pair of them had been out for almost five weeks and he was missing Valerie. He looked over his right shoulder at the navigator's suite. Emmy's gift smiled back blankly. A genuine, right from the company store, Princess Nanamoushki. The toy plush, pink, winged hippo, in a princess tutu with 'magic' holographic projection wand stared back with a saccharine open mouth smile. Thankfully it was a dumb plush toy, not a mechoid playmate or reactive beyond that wand.

To Winston, it was the horror spawn of a marketing nightmare. How many little girl tropes could be checked off at one time? But to Emmy, she would lose her mind and be propelled to the top of her little social circle. Valerie would enjoy some spillover jealousy from the other moms she hung out with while the kids were on play dates. Perhaps he should give her a heads up on what was coming?

He took a moment to check the lag time for video comms. They were close enough to be near instant transmission.

"I think I'll comm Val," Winston announced.

Jeph gave a soft grunt that pretended to acknowledge what Winston said.

The comm purred as he rang his wife.

Valerie picked up, her smile forcing itself through a frustrated grimace.

"Hi Darlin'," Winston chirped.

Before a word escaped her lips, a power ballad of Emmy's familiar shriek and tantrum began off camera.

Winston's lips curled back in a shocked cringe. Valerie's face became an executioner's masque of overwhelmed mama bear.

"Enough! Go to your room!" Valerie shouted at their daughter.

Emmy's rebellious screams off camera were incomprehensible through the snot and tears save for the repeated syllables of "'No', 'want' or 'mine'!"

Behind Winston's disheveled wife, their apartment was a horrid mess. Toys and clothes and unidentifiable clutter were everywhere. Knickknacks, brick-a-brac and tchotchkes littered the apartment. Every trashcan in sight was filled to overflowing. Slowly he realized that most of the clutter was of similar items, the Princess Nanamoushki collection. So much pink.

"Be right back," Valerie finally said and went off camera to deal with the tantrum throwing Emmy.

He could hear the out of sight struggle to scoop up his daughter and the thump of his wife's feet. Valerie marched by the camera to Emmy's bedroom, their screaming daughter slung over her shoulder. The sight of little girl fists hammering on his wife's back made Winston wince. Muffled shouts of admonishment were indistinct, but Winston knew what they were. He'd said them many times himself when Emmy spun out of control like this. The howl of agony mixed with the rage of a little girl denied her power was dampened by the closed door. Yep. Consequences suck, sugar child.

The loud crunching behind him stopped. Winston could feel Jeph's eyes looking over his shoulder at the comm projection.

The crying got loud as Emmy's bedroom door opened again then slammed. Angry feet pounded their way back to the house comm.

Valerie looked ready to burst into tears. Her beautiful chestnut hair up was in a messy, mostly undone bun, her blouse crookedly fastened one button off and covered with a purple stain that looked like jelly. A red welt on her cheekbone was swelling.

"Dare I ask?" Winston said.

"Go on, dare," Valerie snapped.

Winston knew better than to take that bait. She was going to tell him soon enough.

"Your daughter," Valerie began. He knew his daughter was in deep trouble when Valerie referred to Emmy as 'his', not 'theirs'.

"Somehow she managed to get ahold of our credit account and buy the Princess Nanamoushki nanofab collection."

"Oh no," Winston gasped.

"Oh yes!" Valerie said. "See this?" she made a grand sarcastic gesture toward the mess behind her.

"That's what came out before I could stop our nanofab unit. Honestly, it's not stopped, just paused. She clicked accept not just once, but Xiao knows how many times before she stopped. The fab queue is several dozen pages long!"

"Holy cheis! How much did that cost?" Jeph asked.

Winston wheeled around to find his loadmaster unapologetically staring wide-eyed at the comm. "Do you mind?" he shouted at Jeph. "Private conversation here."

"Then don't be screaming about it in the cab," Jeph sulked.

"Can you just-" Winston let out a frustrated sigh. "Just please go to your sleeper for a bit?"

"Purg, yes," Jeph said with a mix of disgust and horror. He popped open his crash frame and headed for the second sleeper, muttering. "What I don't need is some more of your domestic tranquility."

"I'm trying to get the money back, right now," Valerie said.

"How much?" Winston said, now terrified of the answer.

"If they don't give us our money back, we're in the hole several thousand this month. I'm not sure what I'll be able to do. The Dataoid I was talking to before you called said something about not refunding for what we've already fabricated." She pointed at the piles behind her with a tilt of her head.

"Not to mention the feedstock cost. That's just gone, but we can at least recycle these things. That was what the tantrum was about. I was dumping a trashcan into the digester. She tried to save one of the dolls and got smacked for her trouble. It would have taken her arm off!"

"Can I make my initial payment on my new tug?" Winston's panic rose.

"Depends," Valerie hedged.

"What do you mean 'depends'? We can't miss this payment!" Winston shouted.

"Don't you take that tone with me, Winston! This was not on purpose. I still don't know how she managed to get the bank access, though with how slippery that dataoid at customer service was, I bet something crooked was going on."

"Nothing crooked was going on. I'm betting you had your password written down where she could find it and her little friends pressured her into doing it. Were they over there today?"

Valerie gave a suspiciously tight smile. "For a couple minutes this morning, yes. Little Lizzy and her mother came by-"

"And you two ignored the girls while you drank wine as usual," Winston judged.

"Are you implying I have a drinking problem?" Valerie reared back, eyes filled with cold indignant fire.

"No! I'm inferring you have a responsibility problem! When Karin and her little brat Lizzy come around you always do this. You two gossip and have wine while Emmy gets pressured into misbehaving because neither of you are watching!"

"You just hate my friends!" Valerie hissed.

"No, I don't *just* hate your friends. I-"

"Oh, yes you do," she interrupted. "I'm sorry. I can't be like you. I don't enjoy being alone all my life!"

"What the purg does that mean? I'm a pilot. I make a living hauling on the lanes. It's not something I can do from home." Winston's shouts rang off the canopy. He could feel his pulse throb in his temples.

"You've never tried to find anything else to do," she sneered.

"That's a lie and you know it! This job pays enough to make our plans possible. We jus-"

Valerie cut him off again. "There were some perfectly good local jobs where you could be home every night."

"And they pay half as much! We'd barely make ends meet even without the tug payments!" In the silence that followed Winston rubbed his eyes as the throb grew into a dull ache.

Valerie's lips were set in a bitter, hard slash. She glared at the camera and right into him.

"Can I make the payment?" Winston asked softly.

"I don't know yet. By the time you get home I hope to find out." Valerie's voice dripped with venom. "I'll fig-"

Both jumped at the sound of a civil defense siren wailing outside. All over Lougahasa the eerie rise and fall pierced through the comm.

"Val? What's going on?" Winston's mouth dried out instantly.

His cab alarms went off, building into a fearful symphony. The Sierra Madre's horn began to blast a pattern of five short and one long tone. Red warning holos began to spin on every screen.

"Val?" He struggled to hear her as he struggled to turn off the cab alarms so he could hear. His lungs felt like frozen, unable to push enough air to speak. She was listening to a voice coming in on the emergency broadcast system that he couldn't hear clearly over his own warnings.

"Oh Xiao, Winston! A Black Void!" He could feel his face drain of color, mirroring hers. "I gotta go! Everyone has to evac, right now! The whole skyland!" Valerie's voice rose to a shrill frenzy as she bolted for their daughter's bedroom.

"Emmy? Emmy!" she shouted, "Come with mommy, baby. We gotta go! We gotta go!"

Winston could hear his wife's frantic running to get their daughter. "My shoes!" Emmy whined off camera.

"We don't have time, baby," Valerie said.

Jeph burst into the cab. "What the behng is going... on...?" The words died in his throat.

Winston ignored him, his world had reduced to the holo projection of his home.

"Valerie!" Winston shouted helplessly at the comm. Streaks of static and choppy pixellated interference began to hit their connection.

"Chingu," Jeph gasped softly.

His wife rushed by, fighting to slip her own shoes on, Emmy clumsily cradled in her arms. She grabbed her purse by the front door, then headed to the garage and their own flier. The unlatched door slowly swinging wide open

"Valerie…" Winston whispered, helplessness choking his words. Another burst of static. He could hear the garage door rising up, and their old junky flier start up. Outside light poured in through the open doors. There was a funny shimmering quality to it like slow water ripples. The mic picked up the sound of Valerie taking off, accelerating hard. It faded into the distant cry of the civil defense alarms, and dogs barking in the neighborhood.

"Winston!" Jeph's shout startled him.

"What?"

"Look…" Absolute horror was carved into Jeph's face as he pointed.

Winston had been so focused on the call, he did not see what was going on in front of them.

The pitch black cloud of the Black Void filled nearly the entire view of his canopy. They were flying right into it!

Purple lightning fractured the sky with every pulse.

A low rumble grew as Lougahasa was consumed before his eyes. One by one the sirens on the comms went silent, destroyed by the cosmic disaster. The camera began to shake. Decorations fell off shelves and shattered. Lamps fell over. With a series of quick blinks the comm link with his home was cut. Winston now saw through the holographic display as the calamity played out before his eyes.

Jeph jumped into the co-pilot chair and trained the telescope on Lougahasa. A menagerie of airships fled the doomed skyland. Winston knew what came next and it was far too late for most of them. Even those who managed to outrun the event horizon wouldn't make it.

"Hit the brakes, Chingu," Jeph said.

Winston didn't react.

"Xiao behng me! We're gonna die if you don't hit the Xiao nahqing brakes!" Jeph screamed.

The profanity cut through Winston paralysis and he threw the tug into an emergency stop. The *Sierra Madre* came to relative station-keeping and the two men watched in awe.

With a bright purple-white flash that portion of the Dream, and everything in it, vanished. The auto dimming canopy saving his sight. Whenthe canopy cleared an empty hole remained in the heavens. Not even ash existed, only a perfect transparent void, surrounded by walls of clouds was all that was left.

But that spherical hole revealed a glimpse of something beyond the clouds. Something even more terrifying that Winston could never seem to remember.

Just for a second, he saw it. Teasing the edge of his consciousness.

"Reverse! Reverse! Reverse!" Jeph screamed. "Get us out of here!"

Jeph's hysterical voice was miles away as he stared into the void. The expanding implosion wave approached at ultrasonic speed. But Winston remained frozen. Everything he knew and loved was gone.

The shockwave hit. The hypersonic winds boomed and roared, tearing his tug to pieces, dragging him down into the crushing nothing.

~~~

Winston woke up screaming Valerie's name, just like he had a thousand times before.
~~~

Deprived of the vices of smoking or drinking to numb the pain, he writhed and groaned in his bunk trapped in the afterimages of his nightmare. It wasn't long before he couldn't stand the repeating memories any more.

Blindly searching for the induction rig, his hand slapped around on the shelf above his bed. He yanked it down on his brow, loaded up Levitown, and dropped in. The green front door of his simulated home opened and he was greeted by the smell of pot roast and potatoes. The aroma calmed his mind and blew away the pain. Here life was simple, safe and perfect, just as he wanted it to be.

5..

Winston puttered in the backyard, trimming the flowerbed's stone hedging, letting his mind drift in comfortable simulated intoxication. A pitcher of amaretto stone sours numbed his thoughts. Val was out enjoying the warm day in her bikini. It was his favorite baby blue. French cut and classy. She lay in the warm glow of the day reading, a drink sweating on the small table next to her sunchair. Emmy ran squealing back and forth through the sprinkler. A happy eight year old girl at play, jumping in the blue wading pool while wearing her favorite water wings with the Fairy Princess Hippo Nanamoushki on them.

The white sky shone with the typical rainbow refractions on a hot day in the Dream. Promising that there was a mythical star somewhere far off where no one could see. It was bright enough to cast dim shade. He'd never felt comfortable with a historical Earth sky. The blinding point of light always irritated his eyes.

"Knock knock, y'all." came a voice as the sliding glass doors rolled open. Billy Joe glided onto the patio. "Just let myself in. I figured you din't mind none.

Val craned her neck around to see the indu. "You're always welcome to visit," she greeted. He looked no different in the instance than in real life, and completely incongruous to the setting.

"What'cha need, Bubby?" Winston said, killing the weedwhacker.

"I gotta hand it to you, Hoss." Billy Joe Bob admired. "This is one detailed instance. You got everything. Even mosquitoes."

"It's amazing that Xiao even conquered the bugs, ain't it?" Winston agreed. "At least you don't have to deal with them."

"Sho 'nuff." Billy Joe said.

Val got up with a drink for their guest.

"Want one?" she asked, holding out a tall glass of the bright orange beverage.

Billy Joe gave Val a huge grin. His smartex face was jovial by design, looking scruffy from all the scuffs over the years of hard work, but the smile always went into the uncanny valley for Winston.

"I don't drink none. Even simulated. It never worked well with my subroutines."

"Anything else I could get you?" Val tried again to be hospitable.

"Honey, enough." Winston said, the words deactivating her hostess subroutine.

Val smiled and went back to her lawn chair and book.

"What do you want, Bubby?" Winston asked after a big swallow of his drink.

"This load. What's goin' on? Our rate confirmation Mother sent us is garbage town. Ain't no way this job's legal." The indu crossed his glittery charcoal arms across his chest, resting on his metal gut.

"Can't say that it is. Can't say that it ain't, either." Winston hedged.

Billy Joe cracked a smile again. "You sly dog. This is dirty as a pig in a mire."

"Care to dial back your charming southern farmboy drawl a bit? It's getting a bit threadbare." Winston asked.

"Sorry, Hoss." Billy Joe said, eyes flickering as he dialed back the personality mod he'd been so enamored with the last few months.

Winston rolled his eyes. "So you have a problem with this?"

"Well... kinda," Billy Joe admitted, a sour expression on his face.

"I don't see us having any other choice. Could be months till we get work. That's assuming that Mother can get the insurance and that that dip-cheis trucker's agent off our back. Otherwise I'm not sure where we can pick up some other work. Mother's going to do her best, but even her hands may be tied. At this point, I just hope we're just bootlegging something mildly illegal, and not something that's a Class 10 gray goo nanodisaster waiting to happen," Winston said. With every reason he felt his face pinch tighter and tighter.

"Just making sure we're on the same page. I don't like it, but what choice we got?" Billy Joe said.

"That's how we got here, Bubby." Winston said, his eyes staring into space.

The two stood there contemplating, listening to Elly's squeals and the sound of dogs barking in the distance.

Billy Joe broke out of the reverie and asked, "So why'd you pick this time in history? You could make anything you wanted. Why not a mansion on some pleasure moon or a penthouse on Metroballis. Heck, y'all could even do a more interesting time in history, not this square box slice of Americana."

Winston shrugged his shoulders and looked at his lounging wife and playing daughter.

"Do I dog on you for your choices in virtual recreation?" Winston said with a grimace.

"I don't go in for these created simulations like this. Seems I lack the imagination," Billy Joe admitted.

"Touché." Winston tipped his glass to his partner.

"You know I ain't doggin' on ya, Hoss. I'm just wonderin'. Even I can appreciate the craft it took to make this. Look here. You got weeds in your tomatoes. That's an attention to detail I couldn't even think of."

Winston considered Billy Joe for a moment, drained his drink in a big swig. "It's a mini-game."

"I suppose this is a peaceful time and place. A time before Xiao and the Dream. When Earth existed and you could trust that the ground you stood on was never going to vanish. Ignorance, sure. Bland? You bet. But it's my zen garden. My raking of rocks or a labyrinth to walk. The home I wish I could have had for real."

Billy Joe nodded his head, feigning or truly understanding for real. It didn't matter to Winston. This was more than he'd ever opened up about his Levitown home instance to anyone.

"Well," We got work to do. I came in to tell you we're coming into control range for Consolidated. I took the liberty of sending a comm, and that string is all staged and ready to go."

"See you in the cab, Bubby," Winston agreed.

The indu vanished in a cloud of sparkling pixels as he logged out.

Winston walked over to Val and sat down on the grass next to her. She gave one of her contented groans, he reached out to stroke her thigh, glistening with oil.

"Love you, honey," he sighed.

"Love you too," Val said, and reached over to stroke his five day beard and run her thumb over his lips. Her eyes were almost hidden behind her shades, but he saw them twinkling, happy. He kissed her hand.

"Back for supper." Winston groaned as he got up.

"Miss you till then," she whispered.

"Me too," he said, and vanished.

Then came the hard myoclonic jerk back into his sleeper.

6.

"Hoss, I really don't like these gauge readings. Pulling ten armored hazmat containers is hard on our baby," Billy Joe said coming back up from the reactor control annex.

"I know, I know. Felt it when making that turn out of the Consolidated yard," Winston fussed back. "Ain't the first time we've pulled this much, though."

The power draw on the Sierra Madre's reactor was staggering when compared to a normal string of containers. The good news was, barring a load of uranium or some other super-dense cargo, the energy draw would hardly change. The bad news was the readouts danced on the dark yellow to orange side of the spectrum with a worrisome flutter. It was tolerable, but if something happened, she'd red-line and scram the reactor or worse.

"The grav relays will need to be stripped and rebuilt after this is over," Billy Joe worried on, seeming to read Winston's mind.

"Nahq, mench!" Winston swore. "Stop with the old mother hen routine! I hate it just as much as you do. I see the same things. We've got maybe two too many cans on our back, but we got no choice."

Billy Joe made a clucking sound with his cheek and tongue.

"Gah! I hate that!" Winston said, squirming.

"Sorry. You know I can't help it when I get overwhelmed," Billy Joe said.

"Didn't we do a thorough check?" Winston sighed.

"Yeah."

Winston started scrolling through the pretrip inspection screen again. "No problems, right? None of the treble grav couplers were flakey, yes?"

"Check, I found nothing wrong," Billy Joe said and sighed.

"All the container's internal gravity planes worked just fine?" Winston kept hammering on his point. They did their job and did it well.

"Okay! I get it. It's just..." Billy Joe paused, letting the silence fill in the rest.

"I'm with you on this, Bubby. I don't like it one bit. We're flying on the ragged edge of disaster, and if anything goes wrong on this run, well...?" Winston sympathized. "If you can give me a better option, I'm pretty sure I'd take it."

"I guess we'll be fine, as long as these containers come back in one piece and everyone plays well with each other and does their part," Billy Joe said, deliberately ignoring the pesky whine of engine alarms. "So, all that matters is that we did our job. If the containers rupture or lose power, well, that'll be all she wrote. We'll be a smear on millions of tons of cargo can, accelerating through us as it falls toward the engine's imaginary black hole until it hits something tougher than us."

Winston gave Billy Joe a horrified look followed by a weary eye roll. He turned to watch the clouds whoosh by and shook his head. "Ain't you just a barrel of laughs."

"Just don't play crack the whip, Hoss." Billy Joe snapped back. Winston laughed despite himself.

~~~

Monte Moncalme was a wedge cut out of a planet like a colossal grapefruit section. The underside consisted of strange icicle shaped peaks and drip-like sandcastles of frozen magma. The outside curve of the skyland's wedge was a taiga of dense mountainous forest. It reminded Winston of a pre-Dream movie he saw shot in the Carpathians about some count.

They arrived right on time as the skyland rotated into her shade and deep twilight fell on the valley. Winston dropped to sub-mach speeds as they followed their cleared flight path into the narrow valleys that hid them from view on nearly all sides. The Sierra Madre's telescope showed this to be part of a private estate.

True night was only something you saw from videos of old Earth. It didn't exist in the Dream unless you got caught in a thick enough cloud or
~~~

went into the shivering cold deeps. Though the narrow valleys looked able to give a close approximation of what the ancients called astrological twilight.

"Billy Joe," Winston asked. "See what you can get on the local net about this place. I really hope we're not being suckered."

"Rog that, Hoss."

After a few seconds, an auxiliary holo opened up to Winston's left with Billy Joe's findings of ownership, tribal affiliation, Imperial status and favor.

"Duke Justinian Payzhur?" Winston didn't recognize the name, and continued to flip down the data as they entered the authorized glide-path. They were five by five and on the way down.

"Looks like that's Duke Payzhur. Humanist tribe. Member of Xiao's First Court, but not too high a member. Important member of a long list of corporate boards and Imperial bureaucracies. A kissing cousin from a long line of the Payzhur family scattered all throughout human space like an ancient clan of kings, princes and captains of industry. All highly connected and busy getting their cut as middlemen from all sides, while still enjoying the favor of Emperor Xiao." Winston whistled low in appreciation, realizing that not only were they about to do something crooked, it was so crooked, it had to screw its socks on in the morning and then would deny it ever owned socks.

"Working for human supremacists. I don't like this one bit." Billy Joe said.

Winston understood how his partner felt. Billy Joe feared destruction just like he feared death. Even though he was a mechanoid with the ability to be restored from his last save. He would still lose some memory if he was brought back, just like an amnesiac.

"Me too, bubby. Let's just pray that we get out of this with our skin intact, somehow," Winston agreed.

"Hoss, I never wanted a gun so bad," Billy Joe moaned.

"Kinda too late now," Winston muttered, feeling the same way.

Winston oriented the Sierra Madre's train of containers to match the ground as they swooped in to their final approach. From this angle, the thin slice of sky was resplendent with the dark reds and deep purple shadows associated with night. The valley itself was miles long, dotted with Potemkin villages for the amusement of the Duke.

"Look at that!" Billy Joe gasped, pointing down at a set of fantastically ornamented pavilions and latticed rides. "A private theme park?"

"Rich people's toys." Winston said with a chuckle.

The nav beacon's programmed route led further past the palatial manor home in a looping curve, keeping them away from the tranquil beauty of the duke's palatial grounds, and over a less manicured environment with fewer watching eyes.

The servants' quarters and dirty industry necessary to maintain the illusion of bucolic luxury slid below the Sierra Madre as she coursed down a secondary branch of the valley. Several dozen warehouses stood next to a 'we'll look the other way for cash' nanofabrication mill. A nest of derricks and scaffolds of nanofeedstock plumbing spread out from it like a spider's web. On the marked loading tarmac, big industrial mechanoids waited for them to land.

Holographic markers were sent to the Sierra Madre's hud, lighting up a tight curved line where they wanted the containers positioned for the onload. Billy Joe bent the string into the desired coil. With a snort, Winston realized that shape would conceal loading activity from his view from the Sierra Madre's cab.

The comm gave its encrypted incoming message chirp.

"This is the Sierra Madre. Go ahead," Winston answered.

"Sierra Madre, this is ground control. Do not spin down your grav generators. Sync it with the local source and keep your fans running." The man's voice was rich and oily like Winston expected. Part of him wondered if he had a waxed mustache to twirl.

"Rog that, ground control," Winston said.

"Once that's done, open your keel door. Envoys will provide further instructions." Again, that voice made Winston think of some white hatted lawman was about to pop up over the horizon and arrest Mr. Evil Mustache and his top hat too.

"Rog that. Synchronizing fields, keeping drive and fans hot. Beware the tidal wells. They will suck you up," Winston warned.

He shared an embarrassed look with Billy Joe. The memory of the foolish trucker shooting through the fan at Omnifeed still painfully fresh in his mind.

There was a gentle bump and the Sierra Madre and her container consist came to rest.

"Roll down port facing doors only," came the instruction from ground control.

"Rog that," Billy Joe responded.

Within seconds, the sounds of onloading cargo penetrated the cab. Fork loaders moving crazy-fast shot to and from the containers. A dozen yards or so in front of the nose stood a small clutch of people in front of a ground limo, wheels and all!

"Check it out!" Winston marveled, "Now there is rich people's money in action. A ground car with wheels on this small chunk of rock?"

"When you can afford to waste your money, why not?" Billy Joe said enthused with seeing the luxurious vehicle.

"Must be nice. But then again, after this run, we might have enough money to burn for a week or two," Winston said grinning at the thought of this run's big check.

Billy Joe gave a queer autotuned rebel yell in excitement at the coming payday.

A pair of figures began walking toward the keel airlock door of the Sierra Madre.

"Well Bubby, Looks like we got company. Let's go greet 'em nice and hospitable." Winston said popping open his pilot seat's crash cage.

"I'm so hopin' this doesn't go cattywampus on us," Billy Joe fussed.

"We meet them, get our extra instructions and get out of here," Winston said.

"With how fast those lumpers are moving, we could be in the air in another quarter hour or so, judging by the sound," Billy Joe agreed with an expert opinion.

Billy Joe suddenly made that nervous clucking sound again.

"What now?" Winston growled as he got up out of his seat.

"Maybe it's better we don't have guns," he said, stopping Winston at the gangway down to the keel airlock.

"Why'd you say that?" Winston turned to see what caught Billy Joe's eye.

"Look at 'em," Billy Joe said and pointed just as they walked under the nose of the keel canopy glass. "They move like muscle, not money. Something tells me this has already gone cattywampus."

Winston gave a loud exhale and began descending the ladder to greet the pair. "Like we have a choice now," he said, resigned to whatever fate awaited them.

7.

As the keel door folded down to the ground, steps extended out from its back. A couple waited patiently in the worklights. The human male was dressed in a flowing damask frock coat with exaggerated cuffs and gold coin ornamentation. A subdued blue ascot was knotted loosely over a bright white collar and vest with scintillating embroidery that appeared to be an energy dispersion mesh. His trousers were bloused over black ankle boots.

The woman was swallowed up by a vanta-black cloak and hood that brushed the ground. Save for her dark wine colored lips and a smooth porcelain jaw peeking out, she was an eerie silhouette cutout that Winston had trouble telling her apart from the shadows behind her. A tiny glimmer in the inky black of her outfit revealed her hidden eyes.

In their left hands, the pair held large briefcases armored with corundumite that glittered a dull blue sheen in the airlock lights.

"Good evening?" Winston hazarded.

"Good evening to you as well, Mr…?" the man asked. His slicked back hair was long enough to curl into messy ringlets at his collar.

"I'm Winston. This is my loadmaster, Billy Joe Bob," he managed to say smoothly despite the sudden cottonmouth. Billy Joe gave them a howdy and imaginary hat tip to the lady.

"You may call me Mr. Tollman, and this is Ms. Iverson." The man's voice was not the one he heard over the comms. It was a fine tenor who's inflections made Winston conjure up images of a court duelist. "We are your passengers."

"Now wait a minute. The rate confirmation said nothing about passengers. We don't have room!" Winston protested.

"Come come, Mr. Harper." Tollman tut-tutted. "For a load of this value, being done in such a manner, certain securities and assurances must be maintained."

"Cattywampus, Hoss," Billy Joe said in a sing-song sotto-vocé.

Winston only nodded. "I see, Mr. Tollman, then I guess I am going to have to turn down this load."

"You don't seem to understand your circumstances, Mr. Harper." Ms. Iverson interjected. Her voice so sensual it could start a bar brawl. "There is no backing out now."

"Nahq," Winston sighed. He looked at Mr. Tollman feeling the tight grimacing smile grow on his lips. "Signed our death warrants the instant I said yes, didn't I?"

Ms. Iverson's blood hungry smile stretched wide under the sparkles of her eyes. Winston realized Mr. Tollman spoke only for himself.

"Of course not! Don't let Ms. Iverson's prickly manners get to you." Mr. Tollman said with a genuine laugh.

Winston scoffed at Tollman's assurance.

"What good would killing you do?" Tollman asked. "You are ignorant of what our cargo is, and the containers are to be sealed. We will see to that. You have plausible deniability. As long as you keep your mouth shut for the next seventy two hours after delivery, whatever you say will not matter for the job will be done. The generous payment is not so much for the cargo as it is for last minute discomfort... and to encourage your discretion."

Winston looked over his shoulder. Billy Joe gave him a blank look, leaving him to make the call.

"Then I guess we take passengers. I have two seats, but no place to sleep, and this is a five day transit. My sleeper isn't made for refined people like you, so if you want to sleep, we'll have to take turns and hot-bunk it." Winston said.

"We have slept in worse," Ms. Iverson said. "I am sure we can tolerate a dirty bed and sticky pillow for a few nights. Get back to me when you spend a night sleeping in a pile of corpses."

"Eugh!" Winston grunted, unable to contain his revulsion.

"For now, just think of us as chaperons, if you wish," Mr. Tollman added with a polite smile. "Now, shall we be going?"

With a shrug Winston relented. "I guess so. No point in hanging around here if your minds' are made up."

"They are," Ms. Iverson confirmed.

Winston gestured to the open door, and Billy Joe slid ahead to lead the way. Ms. Iverson followed Mr. Tollman. As the lady glided by Winston, her cloak exploded open in a flurry revealing glossy black arms and legs intermixed in the ethereal black of her outer garment. Twin pistols appeared in her hands before her corundumite case hit the ground with a hard clatter.

"Down!" she ordered.

Startled by her warning and violent reaction, Winston tripped over his own feet. There was a series of loud cracks followed the sounds of wasps zipping over his head. Mr. Tollman was on the first step when the fusillade of musket shots hit, his free hand just starting to slide into his jacket.

He never had a chance to draw his weapon.

Two rounds hooked in like wicked curveballs from the surrounding twilight murk and struck Tollman in the back and hip. His body erupted in a spray of blood and offal as the compressed nanoblades expanded to their full size like tumbleweeds made of hair thin razors. The pieces of his vivisected body hung there, tangled in the glittering fibers that hooked into his clothes like a ghastly laundry rack, blocking the airlock with the vomit-inducing sight. With musical snaps of breaking nanoblades, Tollman's armored briefcase fell from the remains of his hands, scratched but unharmed.

Winston was slackjawwed in horror at the scene.

Ms. Iverson continued firing as the hidden enemy now boiled out from their ambush. Dozens of Imperial waroids charged, shooting wild suppression fire at the limousine and the armed mercenaries that had been guarding the onload. Glittering drifts of nanoblade formed razor-like barriers in the wake of the imperial warroid's sprayed automatic fire, cutting off the landing pad. They sparkled like threads of black ice in the glare of the lamps and flashlights.

"In the name of Emperor, Xiao the Eternal, lay down your weapons! Lay down your weapons and surrender!" came an amplified mechanoid voice echoing over the gunfire.

Ms. Iverson seemed to vanish in and out of the shadows, her cloak obfuscating her body as she tumbled and slid between cover. Her twin pistols pounded away with hypersonic cracks. Thanks to the pistol's targeting computers that added just the right amount of massé, her rounds arced around corners in incredibly lethal shots, shattering warroid chassis they struck.

Now heavier shocktroops started to open fire. Quick pulses of Em-Rays flicked out with angry hisses of superheated air and the static-like crackles of frying graphene plating.

Winston had no idea where to go. Imperial waroids with the bright blue Imperial Eye of Xiao symbol glowed everywhere he looked. Dazzling flashes of Em-Rays illuminated men and mechs fighting in all directions. Fewer and fewer mercenaries returned fire on the waroids as the skirmish ground down. Smoke swirled around him from small fires started by Em-Rays, rendering the scene into a nightmarish shadow play.

Eight foot tall behemoth waroids emerged from the dark to walk over the vanquished. Xiao's deadly troops were ciphers of idyllic streamlined humans and possessed beautiful emotionless faces of chrome with dimly glowing indigo eyes. Exaggerated, bulbous limbs connected to an over inflated chest and undersized abdomen, cradling over-sized exotic-looking guns. Winston lay face down and slowly laced his hands behind his head in surrender.

A hand slammed down on his shoulder from out of the smoke, grabbing and tugging him to his feet.

"Come on!" Ms. Iverson shouted at him. Winston flinched and looked right into her perfect pearly teeth set in snarling black lips. A burst of musketballs whizzed by his head, but he was too shocked to move. With her free hand, she picked up her own briefcase from the ground next to Winston then put her lips next to his ear.

"Move it, Billy Big-rigger! They're not taking prisoners!" She shrieked furiously in his ear.

Winston snapped out of his bewilderment and desperately looked for his last remaining avenue of escape, the Sierra Madre.

Like an amazonian warrior, Ms. Iverson threw her heavy case into the glittering tumbleweeds of nanoblades and turned the geometric tangles of razors into dust. Mr. Tollman's remains tumbled to the ground with a wet splat.

"Get us out of here!" she ordered.

Winston bolted into the Sierra Madre. Ms. Iverson scooped up Mr. Tollman's case, hot on Winston's tail. Another volley of those horrible gemballs smacked into the ground near him, their deadly blooms expanding to a mere whisper away. Once inside the airlock he slapped the emergency close, but didn't wait to verify a seal. He could see the gaskets were sliced to ribbons by the remaining nanorazors, but were good enough to show green.

"Bubby!" Winston shouted as he ran up the steep steps to the cab, "Close us up, 'cuz we are leaving hot!"

"Rog that, Hoss!" Billy Joe shouted back.

Winston threw himself into the pilot's seat while Ms. Iverson jumped into the co-pilot's behind him.

"Come on, come on! Do I need to help?" she asked, her voice pianowire tight.

"No! Just keep your fingers off every behnging thing in here," Winston snarled.

"Bubby! Are we ready to go?" Winston shouted, more out of panic than to be heard. A laser shotgun scribbled a burst on the canopy.

"Nahq it!" Winston cussed, and raised the particulate shields. "Gonna have ta do it blind."

Below the cab, monitors showed Xiao's waroids peppering the underside. Their shots only took the paint off. The commercial grade hull of the Sierra Madre was still too tough to be harmed by hand weapons, but Winston was sure they had heavier firepower nearby.

"Lock it and cock it, 'cuz we're ready to rock it!" Billy Joe exclaimed. "Zero buoyancy, Hoss!"

"Let's kick this pig!" Winston shouted back.

The crackling roar of the grav fans obliterated all other sounds. Aimed at the ground, the fan wash cleared the landing zone of all loose matter that weighed less than a few tons. Crates, Xiao's waroids, mercenaries, loader mechs and the limousine were suddenly thrown into the air by the supersonic airblast and the Sierra Madre with her train of ten container's shot skyward, twisting like a Chinese dragon. Their acceleration was so fast that they broke the sound barrier just a few hundred yards from ground, blasting out every window for a mile.

"We did it!" Ms. Iverson shouted, gleefully. Laughing like a kid on a rollercoaster. "Behng me, flyboy! You sure know how to make an exit," she praised.

Winston's mouth was a bloodless cut, lips pressed tight. He doubted Ms. Iverson could recognize the worrisome shake cutting through the Sierra Madre's frame. The power gauges were about to cross the redline and Winston hoped nothing would give out. As they touched max load mark, he eased back the throttle from emergency power and backed it down to full speed. Winston listened closely to the sounds and felt for unusual vibrations. As soon as he was certain that nothing was going to blow up,

Winston flipped over to his cameras, looking for signs of damage.

The container's interior feeds were blocked either by cargo or someone covered up the lenses. He reviewed the telemetry metrics history. No evidence of gravity plane fluctuation during their ascent, so the cargo probably hadn't shifted, but until he could go check physically, it was just a guess. Switching over to the traffic net scanners, Winston searched for signs of pursuit. Xiao's ships wouldn't show up on it, he chided himself. They used coded transponders he couldn't access. The beacon tracks of commercial and private ships were clear.

"Bubby, get on the telescope and tell me if there's anything following."

"You got it, Hoss".

The Sierra Madre broke out of the dusk side of Monte Moncalme. Sometimes the best tool to use to spot someone is the classic 'Mark-One Eyeball' as the old saying would go.

"Maybe we got lucky?" Billy Joe suggested. "Got away in the chaos?"

"That'd have to be mighty lucky, Bubby. Something we have been in short supply of lately," Winston muttered.

"How could anyone catch us now?" Ms. Iverson said. Her prideful tone irritated Winston.

"This is a tug, not a fighter." Winston explained without looking back. "Purg! Any one of their troop transports could catch us. We can only go hypersonic, that means mach twelve to fourteen, tops. Those Imperial ships can crack megasonic speeds. You don't see that near skylands or moons, because the shockwave is so destructive. And the heat from the atmosphere would burn you up. They only use that kind of speed in clear skies. Never in the soup."

"You know your way around the layers of the Dream, don't you, flyboy," her voice, now a sultry purr, was right next to his ear, hot breath brushing his hair. Winston flinched back from her like she was a cobra. He fought to free himself from his crash frame. Flailing wild to get clear of its padded restraints, he staggered forward until he slammed into the nose of the cab in front of the triangle of crew seats.

Ms. Iverson's body was hidden in the folds of that featureless ebony cloak, but her face now exposed for him to see… was stunning. She was on the verge of being a caricature of female beauty. A real life Helen of Troy. Multicolored hair in red, purple and blue streaks rolled down her neck and shoulders in waves, perfect complimentary makeup and lips now an exciting glossy red.

"Wha, what?" Winston failed to form a coherent thought.

She laughed with her sexy, bar-brawl inducing voice.

"You look surprised. Never had a real woman in your cab before? Or just lot lizards?" she teased.

Winston just swallowed, his guts were turning into knots that twisted into even more knots.

Slowly, she stood up, letting her cloak, shredded from dozens of imperial near misses, revealed that the impossible caricature went all the way down in resplendent glossy black curves to the tips of her incredibly impractical heels.

"You can call me Holly, if you like," she said with apparent sincerity. "Thank you for saving me and my employer's shipment from Xiao's little death squad." There was something to her voice that triggered even more feelings that Winston didn't want to have. New knots now went south to parts of his body he'd stopped using since he lost Valerie.

"Hoss, why you acting so squirrely?"

Billy Joe had no understanding of female beauty. Winston could not take his eyes off her glossy black body that looked like violent liquid sex.

"I... uhh... I..." Winston stammered. He felt ripped bare before her and wobbled on his feet. Closing his eyes, he turned his head away. "Bubby, is anyone chasing us?"

"Not that I can see. Sensors won't help us till they get too close to matter anyway. Maybe they were just a local barracks?" Billy Joe reported.

Winston opened one eye, carefully refusing to include Ms. Iverson in his field of vision and started sliding around the outside of the cab like a dog sneaking by a mean cat, trying to avoid a fight.

"My, you are skittish. Don't worry, I won't bite." Ms. Iverson laughed at Winston's move to escape. "But I do nibble aggressively." With every word she spoke, that tantalizing itch in the back of his brain inflamed his animal side which bellowed that he take her... now.

"Good... Bubby. Very... um- good," he stammered. "Just set the autopilot a-and we'll be on our way to delivery. I just- just... I just need to-" and with three big steps Winston flung himself into his sleeper, slammed the door and locked it with a huge sigh. It had been a cheis day, and he couldn't take it anymore.

"What the purg?" Ms. Iverson's voice was outraged.

"Don't ask me, ma'am. I just work here," Billy Joe said.

On went the induction rig, and Winston dropped into his domestic tranquility where he made frantic love to Valerie. Then, he drank till his scrambled emotions and thoughts drowned.

81.

Winston left his home instance thankful that simulated alcohol didn't come with hangovers, but unfortunately the stimulation of those parts of his cortex from simulating heavy drinking could cause disorientation akin to waking up from a deep sleep. Unable to order his vague recollections of what was going on, he scratched his scalp, pantomiming his search through fuzzy memories. Where were they again? Did they drop at Omnifeed?

Standing with a groan, he slid the door open on the sleeper and found himself face to face with one very irritated looking Ms. Iverson.

"Pardon me," she said. With two glistening black fingers on his shoulder she guided him out of her way. "I've needed to powder my nose for several hours now, thank you."

Evicted from his sleeper by a beautiful woman he could not quite remember, Winston looked around the cab, a bit unsteady on his feet. Billy

Joe stood by with a disappointed expression. Winston hooked a thumb at the sleeper door as a question to his loadmaster.

"You tied one on virtually, din't you, Hoss? How much did you fake drink? Even your eyes are bloodshot," Billy Joe grumped.

Winston couldn't make the connections.

"That is our passenger, chaperone or whatever you want to call her. She came with the cargo we're haulin'," Billy Joe further explained.

"Gonna need a little bit more than that," Winston said, rubbing his itching eyes.

"For the ten containers of cargo we're hauling like a bat outta purg to a place we ought not be for a paycheck that ain't exactly legal?" Billy Joe snarled.

"Ohhhhhh..." Winston said as he remembered Mr. Tollman. "Eugh!" He rubbed some of the sleep out of his eyes. "Can you blame me though? I'm not used to that kind of violence."

Billy Joe only shrugged. "So now what, Hoss?"

Winston went over to the pilot's seat and tapped open some screens.

"We weren't followed so far as I could tell. We were lucky to end up in a sand storm for a few hours which blew us off course a bit. Nothing the autopilot couldn't correct for but may help cover our tracks."

"Well you know the old saying, 'if they don't chase you after the first thousand miles, they're not interested in you'," Winston quoted the old pilot's homily.

"Yeah, but dat don't make sense. Not with how they came in loaded for bear."

"Bubby?"

"Yeah?"

"Stop looking that gift horse in the mouth," Winston sighed.

"Well I kept an eye out, and they din't follow that I could tell," Billy Joe said.

"Well praise Xiao," Winston said, dismissing the worry. "She didn't mess with-" he started.

"Never touched a thing. Asked to go back and check the cargo. I said no, 'cuz we ain't slowin' down till you wake up, and I wouldn't let her in your sleeper. Since then, she's just been pacing off and on. What the purg got into you?"

Winston looked at his clock. He'd been asleep for ten black hours.

"She hits a nerve, okay? Maybe literally. Every time she spoke it was like a part of my brain that wasn't supposed to itch started itching," Winston struggled to explain.

"Huh. Sure you weren't just horny for the real thing?" Billy Joe understood that much about biological life.

"No!… Yes? I don't know," Winston looked at the deck. He did know, and lying to himself made it worse. "Maybe!" For the first time in twelve years he even wanted sex in the flesh with another woman. It sure explained what he did with Valerie when logged in. It wasn't even good. It only relieved that itchy brain sensation and not much else. No true pleasure and definitely no love.

The door to the sleeper opened, and Ms. Iverson walked out. Winston shot up out of his pilot's seat.

"What the purg did you do to me with your voice?" he snapped.

"What?" she asked hovering between acting innocent and haughty. The cognitive dissonance in Winston's brain became even more powerful.

"My brain was twitching when you talked. Was that some sort of neural scrambler or some freaky sex toy for the ultra wealthy? If so, knock it off! I'm a happily married man!"

She crossed her arms, popped out a hip and glared back with equal hostility, but said nothing.

"Well? Got anything to say for yourself?" Winston demanded. "Anything at all? Hmm!?"

"I must say you are the first man I've ever run across that could both appreciate a woman, but get angry at a subsonic limbic manipulator. Most men are reduced to putty by my little purrrrrrr..."

Winston felt that itching in his brain and stirring down below again as his body involuntarily reacted to her sultry voice.

"Behnging purg! What did I just say?" he shouted, and stepped almost nose to nose with her, forgetting that this woman, despite her appearance, was probably a wired assassin or bodyguard of some kind. "Knock it off," he rumbled and then shoved a finger in his ear to itch as she let out a little chuckle.

"Hoss, maybe you should cool off. It's not like she's doin' you harm," Billy Joe said.

"Better listen to your Bubby, flyboy. I don't mean to hurt you none," she sighed, copying Billy Joe's southern accent. "Besides, if I really turned on my full charm," she said as she walked around him to the front of the cab, lightly tracing a sharp armored fingernail on his chest, "you'd be mush before you knew it."

Once in the nose of the cab, she struck a taunting pose right out of a porn network. "But, I'll play nice… at least for now." This time Winston's brain didn't itch. A huge pressure seemed to lift from his chest and he breathed in relief.

"You better," he snapped.

"Threats not withstanding," Ms. Iverson said changing subject, "Time we inspected the cargo since it wasn't properly done before we left thanks to Xiao's rude interruption."

"Nah," Winston countered. "I need to clean up first. I feel nasty."

"Now, wait. I let your attack toaster keep me from checking earlier, but I won't be put off anymore. I need to make sure we're getting there with all the pieces and parts," Ms. Iverson retorted. "People who make such purchases aren't always known for their good sense of humor."

"Ma'am," Winston complained, "Twenty minutes ain't gonna make any more difference now."

"Why's that?" she demanded, fists on hips. Winston gave her a world weary gaze through his sleep-sand encrusted eyes

Billy Joe slid partially between them, heading off the fight. "'Cause we've been flying at full speed for over ten hours now. Any door that wasn't sealed is probably long blown open. 'Dat means anythin' that wasn't secured against mach twelve winds is gone. Sucked out through the open door."

"And with Xiao's death squad possibly after us, there's no way we're going back for it even if we could find it," Winston finished his partner's thought, peeking over Billy Joe's shoulder at her.

The space between them grew in the silence, punctuated only with the occasional rattle of the Sierra Madre's supersonic flight and the air-conditioning's hiss.

"Make you a deal," Winston offered as he stepped around the pair and knelt down next to the pilot's seat. He opened the meteorological scanner. "Let me..." he tapped a few icons on the holo display, "find a place..." spread his fingers out on a detected cloud bank and enlarged the image, "...for us to park. Then we'll go look."

He stood up, arms out, looking for her approval.

"Fine," she muttered.

"I'm going to take that shower now," Winston said and walked past the wired assassin.

Ms. Iverson gave a nasty smile and fired one last dig over her shoulder, "Do you want som-"

"No!"

9.

By the time Winston exited the shower, he felt more like himself.

His dirty flight suit was being washed and he changed into a clean one. It was nice to be in fresh clothing. The shave was a treat. Smelling the aftershave drew out memories happier days.

Stepping out of the sleeper, he noted Billy Joe wasn't there, but Ms. Iverson was in the navigator's chair dozing or listening to music. Her leg bobbed to an unheard beat. He stood entranced by the movement of those crazy tall heels, but then noticed her hair was a mousy blond, tied back into a simple braid. Winston cleared his throat.

"All done?" She looked up and back at him. "My! You do shine up nice," she said with a smile.

"What's that supposed to mean? Are you going to start in on me already?" Winston recoiled.

Ms. Iverson's face went hard. "Nope. Nope. Flyboy wants to be a monk, that's on him," Ms. Iverson said, holding up her hand as if swearing to tell the truth.

"And what's with the color change?" Winston asked, pointing at her hair with subtle flicks of his finger as if to tease it at a safe range from across the cab. Her makeup was very plain now, lips a light pink, and a trace of mascara.

"Are you some sort of a rube, too?" She laughed, looking at him incredulously. "Grooming nanos and embedded mutable makeup, flyboy. They're better than a full-time aesthetician. Fully customizable hair too," she added as her hair flared through all the colors of the visible spectrum. "It even curls or straightens as I want. Best toy for a wired girl ever."

"Ah," Winston said with a nod. "Must have cost a mint."

"You've no idea how much coin it took to cultivate my appearance. Even nature needs help to achieve perfection." She let her makeup fluctuate a moment to something far more exotic, then went back to being plain.

"All fake then," Winston said, flatly. "Compensating for being an ugly teenager?"

"Fake? Compensating?" she rose up like a djinn from a broken bottle. Her reply was a venomous fume.

"Yeah, store bought beauty. Not the real thing." Winston said, savoring a bit of schadenfreude that he double-tapped her soft spot.

"And this is bad how? You don't see a beautiful building or skyship and think that it's beauty is fake, do you?" Ms. Iverson's arms waved in broad, angry sweeps.

"Those are just things, not people," Winston stated.

"There is no difference," Ms. Iverson snarled. "Beauty is beauty. Whether you won the genetic lottery, squeezed it from a tube, cut for it, had a surgeon implant it, or had an engineer bolt it on! I am beautiful," she blasted back.

Winston remained unimpressed.

"Hey!" She poked him on the chest, hard. Hard enough that Winston thought she left a hole. "My look is not by accident! I chose to look this way for my work, and, Flyboy, let me tell you, I have never had a man that I couldn't handle nice and peaceful because of it! Every curve and color. Every cut of clothing is for a purpose, and that is to protect me! I use scientifically proven psychological triggers to keep men docile and women intimidated! And it works like a charm!"

"Except on me," Winston said with a grin.

"Gorgon cheis! Even on you, Flyboy! Who had to run from the cab to get away from my power? And that was just with my voice and looks? Xiao help you if you even got lucky enough to kiss me, let alone behng me! Which, by the way, is off the table!"

Winston fought to keep from laughing at her outburst. "After spending so much time and effort trying to seduce me?"

"I'd rather behng your Bubby, first," Ms. Iverson shouted.

"Happily married, remember?" he lied. "And you couldn't have gotten me so worked up without your tricky neuro-manipulating vox, and what else? A pheromone spray? Some sort of lethal aphrodisiac? What other pharmaceutical trick would you have to pull to get me out of control with desire?"

Her face went bright red and she whipped out her pistol pressing the nearly inch wide muzzle hard to Winston's temple.

"How about this little sex toy, hmm? I could empty your brainpan without a second's remorse," She growled, lips trembling with anger.

Winston was surprisingly calm. "And then what? Do you know how to pilot the Sierra Madre? Got many hours in the pilot seat of a commercial tug? This ain't a runabout or private yacht. You screw up buoyancy or planar shear and you're a smear on the front of a container."

Her lips were black again making her pretty canines seem all the more fierce. Even her irises were fluctuating between blood red and black and her face drained to a porcelain white mask.

"Are the mood eyes and lips a feature or just poor coding on the nanites? Must be difficult to work with that handicap giving your true feelings away," Winston taunted.

"You like playing with fire, don'tcha?" her voice was a hoarse whisper.

"I got nothing to lose. It was taken away by lots of different people, you're just the latest in line... but I know you need me alive." The admission was somehow liberating. All his conflicted feelings became spinning eddies in his wake. Like busting out of a cloudbank into a bright clear layer of the Dream.

"Y'all playing nice up here?" came Billy Joe's voice as he cautiously slid up the ladder from the keel airlock.

Ms. Iverson sharply pushed Winston's head with the gun, re-holstered it and gave him her back.

"I think so," Winston said, rubbing at the dent the muzzle ring left. "Where were you?"

"Cleaning up all those nanorazors in the keel. You'da been cut to ribbons if you went down there without armored workboots," Billy Joe said.

"Good thinking, Bubby." Winston said. "I don't know about y'all but I think it's high time we checked that our cargo is secure like responsible little professionals." He looked at Ms. Iverson with a mocking inviting smile. "Care to join us?"

"Now we're going to do what I asked an hour ago? Fine. If for nothing else than to keep you from stealing anything which will get us killed? Sure," Ms. Iverson sneered.

Winston replied in kind, "Whatever gets you through the day, Lady."

10..

Winston, Billy Joe and Ms. Iverson put on Bumblebees. It was never smart to cross between containers without a flight harness, for even moving at dead slow speed, a surprise crosswind could tear a person clean off. A reality of which Winston was keenly aware. Every pilot has their own close call story to tell, so better to be safe rather than sorry. The flight harness wouldn't keep them from going 'Dutchman', but would provide a chance, no matter how slim, to return to safety. Otherwise, they would just fall forever until dehydration, starvation or exposure killed them. Of course, they also could hit something else floating out there, hard.

They went through the engineering passage on their way to the container access airlock. Too much yellow and orange, Winston thought, and grimaced at the warnings on the reactor monitors. The grav drive was going to need a serious overhaul once they were done.

"I see the loading crew didn't have time to seal the containers' secondary access, thanks to Xiao's waroids," Winston said as the door opened, revealing the green light on the container's inspection door. "Probably didn't even put seals on the cargo doors either."

"We can fix that, Hoss," Billy Joe offered.

Winston managed to keep from sighing, but couldn't stop from rolling his eyes. "We aren't helping the criminals any more than we were hired to do. Just leave it."

The grav couplers kept a yard-wide gap of empty space between tug and containers to prevent bumping. This made stepping between them a little risky, but more scary than dangerous. The fareing around the tug's couplers was designed to provide a relatively calm eddy of air at sub mach speeds, allowing for such transit between containers if warranted while in motion. He and Billy Joe turned on their deadman beacons that would make sure the Sierra Madre stayed put, just in case they were blown overboard by a wind gust while doing the inspection. Winston offered his hand to Ms.

Iverson, which she took as the three crossed the gap.

Cargo had been loosely loaded, held in place with airbags and load straps, allowing for snug passage between. The automated loading lights flickered on giving off a cool blue-white light. Billy Joe elongated an arm to peel off the packing tape plastered over one of the cameras.

"My Xiao!" breathed Ms. Iverson as she saw the wrapped pallets.

The container was twenty-five yards long, five tall and five wide. All sorts of strange tracking codes were stenciled on the neatly packed cargo. Winston squeezed through the tight gap in the dunnage and went to the manifest pocket on the door. Billy Joe, unable to fit into the same narrow space, stretched out his nanite skirt, and crawled above the crates. He settled down in the gap by the door, joining Winston. Ms. Iverson struggled a bit more. Her bust and bottom were not shaped for squeezing through such tight quarters, causing her armor plates to catch. Winston pulled off a packing list from the document box bolted to the door.

"Yep, they didn't have time to seal the doors," Billy Joe observed."

Winston ignored his partner. "Do you know what these codes mean?" he asked, holding out the manifest sheet.

With a grunt and a snap of rubber, she popped out from between the stacks and looked at the paper. "It's military codes. I can take a guess, about the product, but it's best to look and be sure. Billy Joe, dear, would you mind opening up one of those crates?"

The indu looked a question to Winston who shrugged after a moment's thought. "We're in all the way. Mr. Tollman said it won't matter if we keep our mouths shut."

"If everything shows up, you may as well," Ms. Iverson added. "The raid is our cover story as to why we opened stuff. Besides, I'm feeling curious."

Billy Joe's utility sand arms oozed into the shape of forklift clamps and moved some of the crates to the small space in front of the doors. His last questioning look was met with her anxious nod. Billy Joe reformed his hands into their humanoid appearance and popped the latches open with sharp snaps and clatters.

Inside they found grids of fist sized orbs with spoon-like levers and pins attached to the top. Ms. Iverson looked up from the packing list. "Flywheel grenades!"

"Flywheel grenades?" Billy Joe said, picking one up and turning it over in his hands.

"What the behng are those?" Winston asked.

"Ohh... you are kidding! You don't know?" Ms. Iverson said with a hint of glee. "These are the safest incendiary grenades in existence. Very naughty and dangerous when charged up,"

"So they're not live explosives?" Winston asked.

Ms. Iverson shook her head. With an amused snort she took the egg-like weapon out of Billy Joe's hand and held it up like a teacher to a little child.

"You arm them with an electric generator. They can trickle or flash charge like a capacitor. Trillions of nano flywheels inside store the energy and spin very fast for a long time. As long as those flywheels keep spinning, there's no worries. You could even use them for a battery and drain the charge off in a controlled manner."

"But," she said with a growing mischievous smile, "when you arm the trigger, the flywheels have a nasty trick. They convert all that energy into an explosion. It's like using a length of rebar to stop a spoked wheel. The motion converts into heat per the first law of thermodynamics, the flywheels overheat, break apart and… kablam!" She delicately acted out the explosion with her fingers. "Superheated nanoscopic shrapnel expands into a huge cloud of plasma. It penetrates solids almost as good as radiation. Anything inside the blast-cloud fries in milliseconds. Cooks you like a potato in a microwave."

Winston's lip curled in disgust at the thought, and he flipped through the rest of the manifest. "That's all that seems to be in this container."

"It's like a warlord Christmas in here," Billy Joe grumbled, crossing his arms over his chest into a single fused mass as only nanite sand could do.

Ms. Iverson seemed unable to contain her giddiness.

"Let's check out the rest!" she squealed gleefully.

"Great. I'm just jolly ol' Satan Claus," Winston muttered.

"What is with her, Hoss?" Billy Joe whispered, leaning in.

"I dunno, Bubby, either she's some sort of schizoid about this stuff or she's making plans of her own," Winston said softly, as Holly went on ahead.

With no other option but to press on, he glumly followed with Billy Joe right behind. The trio passed through to the next container and found more grenades, mortars and other heavy weapon ammo. No wonder they wanted armored hazmat containers. In the third, they found ammo boxes full of musket balls with markings Winston had never seen before.

"What are these, Ms. Iverson?" he asked, holding it up.

"Call me Holly. This Ms. Iverson stuff is too formal for my tastes," she said while rummaging through some packing.

"If you insist. What are these, Holly?" Winston said again, holding up the sphere between his index finger and thumb like a marble.

She came over and took a quick look at the intricate hairline patterns cut into its surface.

"That's a Geometric Expansion Munition, or GEMball. Just like the ones that exploded Mr. Tollman," she shrugged.

Winston almost dropped the round in shock, and put it back in the box with the greatest of care.

"It takes a lot more than dropping it to crack one open. A little safety precaution. But these," she said looking in another crate, "are the really nasty ones. They're nicknamed 'blenders', because they torque as they expand. Turns just about everything in their radius into a smoothie. We can be glad that Xiao's death squad didn't use 'em."

"Why would anyone make such things?" Winston gulped.

"People need killing from time to time. In this case," she tossed the round up, bumped it off her inner elbow and caught it again. "It's better killing through geometry."

After three more containers packed with ammo and four packed full of various types of long arms and heavy man-portable energy weapons, the last container carried some very different crates. They were strange, long, armored crates, almost like coffins stacked on end, packed tight. All of them carried hazmat warnings like you saw on industrial nano-fabricators, that made the hair on the back of Winston's neck stand up.

"What? What is this? Holly? Why am I seeing disassembler warnings? Are these disintegration charges?" Winston's eyes were practically bugging out.

Billy Joe reached around till he found the container's data sheet and pulled it off, handing it to Holly. It was a dense grid of numbers and cargo codes. "What're we hauling?"

"Yeah, gimme a second," she griped. Unhitching the buckles on her generous tactical rig, she untangled herself from a load strap her breastplate hooked. Once free, Holly came around and grabbed the sheet, and scanned.

"Q Staves!" she breathed bringing her hands to her mouth in awe. "By the thousands!"

"Holly, assume I've never been in the military and don't know what the purg a 'Q Staff' is," Winston huffed.

"It stands for Quartermaster Staff, dip-cheis. You can make instant supply dumps with one of these," Holly gushed. "Look. They're about two yards tall with a pill shaped scanner and nanofabrication seed at the top. It makes a scan of the local area for feedstock quality, which may be several hundred yards in radius. Anything in that sphere, living or dead, can be broken down and converted into the pre-programmed stockpile manifest. Then it fortifies and organizes the location into a supply dump with berm and camouflage. We're talking a lot of war materiel, too. Guns, ammo, everything! Even food and basic medical supplies. One of these can supply an entire platoon for a month!"

"Well I'll be dipped. That's why the disassembler warning," Billy Joe drawled unhappily.

"You can have Q Staves that make drones and waroids, armored vehicles and more. I've seen a leaked test video of one of these making an entire fighter wing."

"How… how fast? I mean, how many weeks does it take to do this?" Winston was incredulous. Nanofabrication might be fast in a controlled setting, but in the wild? With so many variables? Impossible.

"Hours." Holly said. "Xiao has been known to use waroid versions of these as weapons. He drops one into a rebel camp in weapon mode, and it goes to work. Once the nanofabricators are released, there is almost no stopping it till they're done. Any enemy in range starts dissolving in seconds as they're broken down and converted into nanofeedstock. The first production run takes maybe five minutes. It makes drones designed to protect the bigger, later assets. When they're finished, they attack the enemy who weren't turned into war materiel."

"Sounds like a horror movie." Winston's mind whirled, looking at the crates like he was seeing thousands upon thousands of dangerous alien eggs, poised to destroy all life.

Holly shrugged. "I guess. If you're on Xiao's bad side."

The three stood there for a long moment, looking at the crates. Winston's face was a tense rictus. Visions of a dissolving school danced in his mind. Boys and girls being transformed into waroids, drones, guns or even food played out in his imagination. The thought of Emmy being disassembled made him smack his lips in an effort to control his nausea. He looked at Holly's face.

Her eyes gleamed with greedy joy.

"Do you know the street value of one of these cases is? Let alone all of them? Boy, I knew our employer was rich and powerful, but this gives me a whole new appreciation for him."

"Nope!" Winston finally shouted. "Everyone out. We're cutting this loose. I won't haul such a... a... an abomination!" He yanked the packing list from Holly's hand, stuck it back on the case and began pushing her and Billy Joe toward the door.

"What?" Holly's face scrunched up with irritation as Winston rudely laid hands on her.

"Out, out, out!" Winston ordered. Billy Joe allowed himself to be pushed forward without protest, but clearly confused.

"I will not be responsible for a gray goo disaster or any of these things killing innocents, let alone dissolving whole skylands or moons!"

Holly spun around, deftly twisting Winston's arm, locking it behind his back, his fingers twisted back enough to touch his neck. He let out a strangled shout, but still struggled to break free.

"Hey, Flyboy! Listen up," she ordered. Winston ignored her and used his extra weight and almost broke out of her hold.

"Nahq, you're wriggly!" she said as his sweaty wrist slipped in her rubber covered fingers. The two grappled and slid through each other's grasp in the tight confines between the crates.

Losing her grip, Holly swept Winston's legs out from under him. He dropped face down with a bang. She quickly straddled his pelvis, sitting on his lower back with her full weight. Billy Joe made a move to free the thrashing Winston from under her, but before his outstretched arms could reach Holly, she scruffed Winston and pinned his head to the floor with her pistol. He let out a surprised yelp of pain as she ground his cheek into the dirty metal. "Get back, lumper!" she shouted, "or I'm scrambling his brains!"

Billy Joe backed off, hands up in compliance.

Winston continued to struggle.

"Calm the behng down!" Holly ordered.

The pressure of the muzzle became intense to the edge of crushing Winston's temple. A ring of icy fire bloomed and he was sure the pistol would push through his skull. He let out a frustrated cry and froze hands out, fingers splayed in surrender.

"Now," Holly growled, gave a loud sniff, and cleared her throat. "Let me explain something to you for the last time. Like me, you're in for the duration of this game, got that... Winston?" She put extra menace on his name. "You think you're all tough right now. Think you got nothing to lose? Nothing that can be taken from you? You're wrong. I know you better than you think."

"Miss Holly, he don't mean nothing," Billy Joe pleaded. She glared back at him, and he got the hint, and mimed zipping his lips.

"We've needed to have this little talk since your tantrum on Mont Moncalme. Tollman was the nice cop. I'm not. He was in charge then, and he had a lot of tolerance for high-horse moralizing idiots because you don't understand how power in the Dream really works. Your right to say 'no' ended the instant you showed up in Duke's Payzhur's airspace. Now, you're going to be a man of your word and see this through. If you do a good job, and keep your trap shut, we'll all go our separate ways, and you'll get paid."

"Then go ahead and kill me," Winston growled through gritted teeth.

"False bravado won't cut it with me, family man," she mocked, shaking her head. "I've got a micro-expression app scanning your face all the time. You think you want death, but you're just another coward. Otherwise, why would you be hiding in your little fantasy world." She paused, letting the words burn into Winston's psyche.

For emphasis, she turned up her limbic manipulator to color her voice. "But you are right on one point. I do need you for the moment. We could have done this the easy way, with money and kept it strictly business. Do the deed, drop and go, then forget we ever saw each other. But that ruffled your self-righteousness. So I offered you the fun way. We could have had some laughs, behnged a lot and you'd have had something to brag about to your pals. Would have been a memorable little five day trip for you, but you had your Xiao nahqing goofyass waifu fetish gumming up that option. Gave you delusions you're all noble and cheis."

After a long contemplative pause, Winston felt the shift of his captor's weight as she leaned down, her lips brushing his ear. Hot breath reminding him that she was a woman of flesh and blood. Holly whispered as tender as a rose petal, her limbic manipulator at full blast, "All for a simulation of a wife and daughter that can't love you."

Those words, with the brutal might of her subsonic vocal augmentation behind them, obliterated the fortress of denial that Winston had constructed against the truth. Valerie and Emmy weren't alive. They were just digital ghosts to numb his survivor guilt. His eyes burned as tears were pressed out by the weight of her words. His hand spasmed an erratic tattoo on the deck with his fingernails. The carefully nurtured lie to control twelve years of anguish was now impossible to maintain. Winston struggled to resurrect the delusion again, but the truth, like a rampaging kaiju enraged by years of repression, rose from the sea of his subconscious and slaughtered Valerie and Emmy in front of his mind's eye again, and again, and again. No matter what he tried to tell himself, they were dead.

A low shuddering moan escaped his lips.

"So, let's talk about threats. Killing you creates more hassle than what I want right now. Therefore, If you fail to do your job or behng with this mission I'm going to motivate you with pain. That includes destroying what you love most sitting in your sleeper."

A cold sweat burst from his pores. "No!" Winston choked out.

"That's right, Flyboy. And if that still doesn't get you to obey, I will hurt you so bad you'll beg to die. You got the picture now?" She flexed her fingers on the back of his neck. The pain was exquisite, and his left arm went numb and felt like it burst into flame at the same time. He mewled like an animal in a trap.

The weight of true powerlessness crushed Winston's will into powder. But then in the silence of surrender, a new sensation, born. From that helplessness, sired by primordial anger, something fresh trickled out of his heart. An understanding grew into an icy flood. It drowned his despair in a rush, washing away the detritus of his destroyed ego and all that was soft and frail, exposing something new. A paradigm shift which was hard and dangerous. His agonized whimpers died away. In the quiet that followed, Winston found some long-elusive peace to survive.

"Okay, you win," he said, his eyes now dead, resentful marbles.

"How about you, big boy?" Holly said looking to Billy Joe.

"I'm all for getting empty and getting loooooong gone," Billy Joe chirped, clearly happy to make it out of this mess alive.

"Good," Holly said, satisfied. "Winston, I'm going to let you up in a second. You understand the real stakes, now. Right?"

"I do," Winston said. His voice had become a chilling revenant.

"I want to get paid, too. From here on out, let's make this as an uneventful ride as possible, all right?"

The pressure came off the side of Winston's skull, and Holly's rose up from his pelvis. His lower back was grateful at the removal of her weight. Slowly, he stood up and stared at this dangerous woman. Electric green eyes analyzed his expressions as she waited for him to speak. Did he see a flash of surprise as she read his face?

"Let's get this job done then," Winston agreed, wiping dirt from his face. He began to squeeze between the rows of cargo, going back to the cab and paused to look at the other two. "Y'all coming?"

111..

A nightmare blasted Winston awake within minutes of dozing off in the pilot's seat. The door of the sleeper slammed open and Holly came out, gun in hand.

"What was that?" she exclaimed.

Winston's legs were stiff as rods, shoving him deep into the cushions. A hand plastered over his heart as it jack-hammered away. The other, a white knuckled claw, dug into the armrest.

"Nothing to worry yourself about Miss Holly," Billy Joe drawled, blinking himself online. He unhooked himself from his alcove rack and let himself down from his hooks as if nothing important happened. He circled the cab in a quick check of the instruments. "Hoss just gets the night terrors from time to time."

"Like he said, don't worry about it," Winston attempted to reassure her through slowing gasps.

"Huh," Holly grunted and reholstered her pistol. "I feel like I should."

Winston carefully got up out of his seat with a groan, and shuffled toward her.

"'Scuze me," he mumbled and pointed at the sleeper door indicating his intentions. Holly got out of his way, a quizzical look on her face.

Winston fumbled about on a shelf above his bunk, grabbed his induction rig headband. On the way out, Winston opened the small reefer, picked out a bottle to drink and a meal bar. His arm brushed against Holly with a squeak as he slid past her in the doorway and plopped back into the pilot seat. "You don't have any clothes other than that dolly armor, do you?" he asked.

"You wear anything other than that grubby flight suit?" she fired back.

He looked back at her with a dead-inside stare and took a chomp out of the meal bar, "touché."

She shook her head as he washed it down with a nutrient shake. Winston checked their navigation and gave a satisfied grunt. Dropping back into the pilot's seat he opened the comms while putting on his induction rig.

"Don't you dare try to link outside this tug!" she scolded. "We don't need a hint of where we are hitting the network."

"I'm not," Winston said, with bitter insolence. "How stupid do you think I am?"

"Very. You sure use that thing a lot," Holly said as he logged in to the mainframe, calling up the connection to his Levitown instance.

"People stay jacked in 24/7. why should I worry?" Winston replied.

"That's with a proper jack or contact points, not with those EM broadcast rigs. They bombard your brain with energy to transfer data. It can burn you up after long exposure, and you clearly get a lot of exposure." Holly scolded, arms crossed.

"You're not my supervisor." Winston said, throwing the meal bar wrapper in a little trashbag on the side of his seat and closed his eyes, pretending to fade away into the simulation.

He could feel her staring at him, and fought the urge to smile. After a moment, he remembered to make it look like he was in REM sleep like induction rigs do to a person.

"He's killing himself, you know," she said to Billy Joe.

"Yes, Miss Holly," Billy Joe said, "and you ain't gonna stop him, neither. I've barked up that tree long enough."

"If he's not going to stop, why don't you push him to get a jack or something? At least the experience of fidelity would be better," she argued.

"Miss Holly, why do you care what he does? A little while back you were ready to put a ball through his brain. Twice," Billy Joe said.

Winston listened to Holly tapping her toe as she considered the indu's insight.

"I don't care about his long term well being," she admitted. "What I care about is his ability to perform. Something he can't do if he gives himself brainburn."

"Hoss ain't done it yet," Billy Joe drawled.

"Impossible. Both of you, impossible," she huffed. Winston heard her throw up her hands and the slap of them dropping against her thighs.

He couldn't hide his smile any longer as he listened to the angry clack of her heels and the slam of the sleeper door.

"Hoss, you playin' possum?" Billy Joe asked. He must have seen the smile. Winston dropped into Levitown to be with Valerie and Emmy again and escape any questions. Even though he found it far less satisfying since Holly stripped his illusions from him, it still was a pleasant way to keep the nightmares at bay.

12.

Since their inspection of the containers four days earlier, the Sierra Madre had not wavered from their upnorthwesterly path. There had been no more conflict between the three sentients as they kept to their own routine and out of each other's way, focusing on sleeping or personal entertainments. Holly on her internal cyberdrive while Winston and Billy Joe used the Sierra Madre's mainframe. The communications suite prudently turned off.

They flew through the less populated skylands of the Dream's upper bands. Major shipping routes were far behind, and the few less traveled ones that remained were bypassed. If anyone was following them, it would be pretty obvious, but if they got into trouble, nobody was around to help them either.

On the fifth day their destination, the moon, Blaugarten, came into sensor range.

"We're here." Winston announced. "You know, I think this is the highest I've ever flown in the Dream." Noting the canopy had polarized twenty five percent and it still felt too bright in the cab. "That's a high Lumen reading! Heat's gonna be unbearable no matter where we go."

Blaugarten's survey scan displayed the moon's map details. The object had heavier than normal gravity, and a close to true day-night cycle as was possible in the Dream. For species built to take the high heat and brightness it would have been a nice place to live, but with the native flora being poisonous and hostile, settlers were contraindicated. Even the oceans were mildly toxic to unmodified human life.

Pharmaceutical firms seemed to love it, Winston observed. Scans also showed some small mining outfits digging for rare feedstock elements, but that was it. A real backwater.

"Well, look at that! Localized weather and its own ocean," Winston said, amused. "That gravity is going to slow the offload." He looked back to see if anyone had paid attention to his comments.

Billy Joe's body hung in his rack, switched off. His mind off in his own simulations. Holly ignored him as she sat in the co-pilot's chair in her own little internal world between sleep and awake.

Winston looked at her stretched-out legs from of the corner of his eye. The pair had been giving each other the silent treatment except where absolutely necessary since his last nightmare. He still could not put a finger on what to think about her thanks to that nahqing limbic manipulator. The fact she was more than happy to kill him, or the promised "worse than death" fate did not help. Winston and Billy Joe communicated mostly through text comms while she kept to her own company. In Winston's estimation, everyone would be happy when this ordeal was over.

Winston looked from those impossible legs to the comm screen and back. If only, if only, he mused. The signal delay to reach Mother was estimated to be over five minutes with the distance and relay lag. They were a long way from home. Realtime data comms were impossible at this range so Winston composed a quick packet.

"Mother. We're checking in at consignee. Had issues at pickup. Need an engine and reactor inspection after containers are dropped off at yard. Load put a lot of strain on the drive and couplers. Please confirm payment. Will advise when empty."

Winston, finger hovering over the 'send' icon, used the cab monitors to see what Holly was doing. Her eyes were closed, swishing back and forth in REM activity. Winston gave a faint, tight smile and pressed the icon. It felt good firing off that message. It was best Mother knew he was almost on site, just in case. Besides, it was too late to stop what was about to happen. At least everything would look normal if questioned by authorities for some reason. Just another pilot contacting his broker on arrival as was standard protocol.

"Do we want to talk about last minute plans on the delivery?" Winston finally said, breaking the silence in the cab.

"What do you think we need to plan for?" Holly asked, reaching her long glistening arms over her head.

"How is this going to work? Normally, I show up and drop the trailers, bump a dock or set her down and let someone unload me. But since these containers are to return with me, I suspect it's going to be a work site with a live unload. Which is it?"

"Don't worry about it," Holly yawned.

"I'm piloting us in, I think I should be in the know," Winston said, stabbing his armrest with a pair of fingers.

"No, you really don't need to," she insisted.

Winston shook his head, disgusted with her attitude. "Care to include us in your plans, just in case?" he demanded.

She got up and stretched her legs, wiggling her ankles like an athlete getting ready for an event. "Nope."

"But-"

"Listen, flyboy. You got us here and didn't give me an excuse to blow your head off. Now, this is my part of the gig," Holly dismissed him.

"What's that supposed to mean?" Winston snapped back.

Billy Joe came awake in his rack, unhooked and came to join in the conversation. "See we're almost at the delivery. What's the plan?" he asked.

Winston made a sharp 'you explain it' gesture toward Holly with both hands indicating his displeasure and the cause of it.

"I've already told Flyboy here, don't worry about it," she explained to Billy Joe.

"So you know how to land a consist of ten containers like this?" Billy Joe asked incredulously.

She ignored the indu's question.

"Speaking of delivering," Winston interrupted. "I think we should ping Mother on this."

"Sounds like a great idea," Billy Joe said.

"Aaah-pup-pup-pup," Holly said in a sing-song warning, pointing a finger sharply at him. "You've been a good boy till now but Mommy's dutiful son is going to get hurt if he tries to call home."

"She's not his real mother, Miss Holly," Billy Joe said.

Holly gave him a sardonic glare.

"The only people we are contacting are the clients. Nothing on the network. Time to let them know we're here," Holly said. Her eyelids fluttered for a moment as she tapped into the Sierra Madre's comm antennae, tightened the beam toward the small moon and fired off an encrypted signal. Suddenly, the tug turned on its approach vector, angling toward the deep jungle.

"Wha-?" Winston yelped as the ship obeyed her.

"Oh please. I've had five days to hack your cybersecurity," she scoffed. "That commercial crap you use will keep most citizens out, but for pros? It's not even a speedbump."

Winston shot her a blazing glare. She smiled.

"After we're done, you can leave me with them. I have other transportation arranged. Then you can scurry back to your mundane existence among the common folk, and do whatever it is you waste your life on, safe in the knowledge you helped out your betters."

"How gracious of you, milady" Winston said in sugar sweet mockery.

Holly glided in front of the pilot's seat and leaned down, putting her elbows on Winston's crash cage, trapping him in the chair with her cleavage front and center.

"I like a man who knows his place in the world, and you figured yours out fast once I explained it to you," she said, tapping his forehead gently with her armored fingernail, tracing a little heart where his third eye would be. "When you square your cheis away, maybe our paths will cross again and we can do some real work for real money. You've got some nice skills hidden in that mess you call a brain, Flyboy, and I'd be curious to see how far you can go and what you really can do."

Winston's face screwed up with frustration. "Is there any time you won't run hot and cold at me?"

She stopped for a second and pretended to think about it, and then to add to the torment she kicked in her limbic manipulator. "No," she said, sensually tickling his brainstem with a laugh. She leaned forward and planted a gentle kiss on his forehead.

Winston pinched his eyes shut. The laughter was as brutal on his libido as was the sweet mockery.

"Thank Xiao this job is almost over," Winston whispered.

"Now, relax. I'm not going to harm your little tug, but you're not flying her for the next few minutes. Your AI is dummied up to ground control, so..." she pulled out her pistol, keeping it pointed at the floor, "hands off the controls, and out of the seat, please," she ordered, lifting up the crash cage.

Winston did what he was told. The thought of rushing her came to mind, but even with Billy Joe, it was a fair bet she would kill them both if they tried. Time to just lay back and think of Levitown.

13.

Blaugarten's northern pole was a rainforest of moss and gargantuan flowers. The Sierra Madre automatically set down among a collection of auxiliary warehouses with smooth efficiency. The whooshing of the grav fans startled a few animals that fled out of holes in the fencing.

"Okay boys, let's finish this game and be on our merry ways," Holly said as the fans spun down and the cab became quiet.

She looked at Billy Joe. "Get my cases." The indu obeyed.

The outside gauges revealed the air was thick but not as hot as Winston expected. Thousands of small creatures began singing again, growing to an oppressive drone as if to show the Sierra Madre they wouldn't be intimidated by her landing.

With a dull rumble, a collection of paramilitarios came out of the rainforest in a convoy of float trucks, pulling up alongside the containers and began disgorging fierce looking, heavily-armed men. From the middle of the string of trucks, a single regally appointed floatcar came toward the keel airlock and stopped.

"Looks like we found the local warlord," Winston muttered to Billy Joe, realizing that any crazy stunt he might have tried to escape vanished with the amount of firepower that just arrived.

"Too right on that, Hoss. Why do revolutionaries always gravitate to tropical places like this?" he whispered back.

Winston just shrugged. "Maybe they watch too many old movies."

"Here we go. Everyone out. Ladies last," Holly commanded, putting her gun away.

"Yes, Miss Holly." Billy Joe responded. Winston just ground his teeth and disembarked.

The passengers in the floatcar were standing about in a sloppy military parade rest. Their leader was standing in front with his aide, looking every bit the part of a tin pot warlord supposedly fighting for his downtrodden people. He was garbed in a resplendent, ornate uniform, and bright orange turban and scimitar. His thick black beard was well groomed and glistening.

As the man in the turban watched them approach, his smile widened, but then fell.

"Where is Mr. Tollman?" the turban wearing man asked.

"Xiao's death squad," Holly said with a shake of her head. "Showed up as we finished loading. He fell in the opening volley of fire."

"Pity. He was a good man," He looked at Winston and Billy Joe. "And these two?"

"This is Winston Harper, the pilot, and his loadmaster, Billy Joe. It would be generous to call them the help, but they managed to be useful somehow," Holly said. Winston ignored the bait.

"They escaped Xiao's death squad with you and the cargo intact, yes?" the man in the turban asked, more rhetorically than questioning.

"True," Holly agreed in a falsely reluctant manner.

"Then they are to be appreciated, for that is an accomplishment unto itself. An Imperial death squad is not something most people walk away from. Even Tollman failed to do so," he declared, then turned to address Winston. "Thank you for helping to free the Dream of Xiao's wretched system of control. You've done more than you realize."

"You're uh… welcome?" Winston said. A grimace tightening his face.

The man stepped forward, his hand out in greeting. The warlord smelled of sandalwood and cedar as Winston took his soft, manicured hands. "I am Count Gustavo LaBlanc of Calliero. I lead these freedom fighters against Xiao's tyranny," he gave a broad gesture to his men who were just as deliberately rag-tag as he was opulent. Right out of central casting. Winston had seen on a newsfeed some stories about the Calliero cluster. It was a long way from here. "We can always use more good mench in this war to end the tyranny of Xiao."

"You'll have to forgive me, Count," Winston puzzled. "I don't know much about the war against Emperor Xiao. In my life, well, he doesn't seem like much of a problem to me. No more than a crooked revenuer collecting taxes and demanding a tip for your trouble. Only big people with baronies, duchies or unions have big problems with him. If you'll beg my pardon on that, sir."

LaBlanc gave out a booming baritone laugh that rocketed up from his belly.

"Spoken like a true peasant! Innocent in your ignorance," he exclaimed. "Oh, no offense intended of course. I can tell you are not one of my subjects. You seem like one of those poor jaded souls of the Union, deceived into believing you were free. At least my serfs know their place in life and my love for them. I find it a much more honest system."

"None taken. I've been reminded of my place in life more than a few times recently," Winston said, looking over his shoulder at Holly. "I know I lead a relatively small and simple life," he agreed. There was no point taking offense at this noble's arrogance. He knew nothing of Winston's life.

"No interest in a more meaningful role? Could I tempt you with serving those who value daring, loyalty and action?" the Count asked with a smile that made Winston certain it was a genuine offer.

Winston looked back at Holly. Did he see an almost imperceptible nod, or was his imagination playing tricks on him? Nahq, that limbic manipulator! Was this Count LaBlanc her real employer, or Duke Payzhur? Did she really want him working with her? What game was she running?

Billy Joe wasn't much more help, giving only a shrug. He was along for the ride, making this Winston's choice alone.

"Not really," he said with a sigh, "This was the adventure of a lifetime. More than I would ever desire again," Winston said humbly. "I just want to live my life free of complications and live in peace."

Count LaBlanc nodded, clearly amused by Winston. "It is good that we hired such an incurious peasant for this job."

A quartermaster came up with a tablet in hand. "My leige, the cargo was unsealed, but our survey shows it is all accounted for."

"Due to your rushed departure, I assume?" LaBlanc asked Holly.

"Yes, Count. We only inspected to make sure nothing was lost during the escape."

Winston hid his surprise at her honesty.

Excellent." The Count smiled. "Now Mr. Harper, would you like to see what you have brought me?

"Honestly, I'm not that curious. It's been strongly suggested the less I know, the better," Winston said.

"Oh, come now. Consider it a reward for your brave service to aid the forces of freedom!" He raised up his sleeve and tapped his wrist. "Bring up a Q Staff."

Winston's stomach soured and his tongue felt like it curdled. Why did everyone keep giving him mixed signals? Is everyone incompetent? Or are they all playing some other game under the table? He was fast getting sick of all the intrigue and wanted nothing more than to return to his uncomplicated life.

There was a quick affirmative response and seconds later the loadmaster came up with a two yard tall Q Staff and handed it to the Count.

"I'm in the mood to have some fun. Yes, yes! Let's see what this can do, shall we?" LaBlanc said like a boy ready to open a present.

Winston, flinched as the on top of the staff was activated. He was ready to jump out of his skin as the small screen began scanning where they were as the best location for feedstock, sweeping across his tug. He looked up at the Sierra Madre. Count LaBlanc saw that and chuckled.

"No no, Mr. Harper. I am not like Xiao the Star Eater. I would not destroy your tug carelessly."

Winston nodded and swallowed hard.

Pointing the Q Staff at a warehouse, "Ah, That will be an excellent place," the Count said, and began walking towards it. His men politely, but pointedly enforced the invitation to join LaBlanc. Ahead, a large hangar door was forced open and LaBlanc walked into the storage facility full of various supplies, replacement parts and mothballed equipment for some of the pharmaceutical labs on Blaugarten.

"My new toys deserve an audience! You and your partner will do in a pinch, Mr. Harper. Not to mention outfit a platoon of my men with Xiao's best equipment," he announced.

"Hoss, we gotta get away from here." Billy Joe whispered.

"I'm all out of ideas," he hissed back.

"My liege," Holly said, "You will be overflowing with equipment for the trucks you brought. Do you really want to waste this here?"

LaBlanq gave Holly a scheming smile. "This is all part of a bigger tapestry, my dear."

"Can this wait until we finish our other exchange?" Holly asked, a hair's breadth from pleading.

Winston noticed her subtle head tilt toward the pair of cases Billy Joe dutifully carried for her. What was she up to now?

LaBlanc gave her a teasing smile.

"That can wait for a more private meeting. This new toy is much more exciting at the moment. It shouldn't take too long," he said as he balanced the staff on end and pulled the mounting trigger. There was a cracking sound as the device punctured the fibercrete with a giant piton. A small plate flipped open beneath the programming interface and a musical warning chime came on.

"Here we go!" the Count breathed, his eyes dancing like a child on Christmas morning, and pressed the stereotypical shiny red button.

The warning jingle changed to an angry rising and falling wail. A spike of terror went through Winston's head. He recognized the sensation of a limbic manipulator, but this one was set to terror. Everyone bolted, clearing the warehouse in record time.

"A fear generating alarm that encourages you to vacate the area. That's thorough," the Count said in appreciation, then chuckled as they panted for breath from running.

Doubled over and gasping from the all-out sprint, "How's it feel to be on the other end of one of those yourself?" Winston said with a laugh at Holly followed by a cough jag.

"Shut the behng up, Flyboy," Holly snapped back.

Winston's eyes fell on her boots.

"By the by, how can you run like a sprinter on the track in what I suspect are seven inch heels?

Is that all cybernetics?" He asked, pointing at her enigmatic footware.

She raised up a foot and smiled in appreciation. "They're very good boots," she said running a finger around the decorative buckles on her thigh. "Gyros for stability and balance, reinforced smartex muscles to protect and enhance my leg strength and an adaptive sole as comfortable as any running shoe. It's impossible for me to sprain an ankle or knee in these. The fact that I have two literal stilettos on my feet and my ass looks fantastic is just icing on the cake." Holly gave a sly smile. "Very practical impractical footwear for my line of work."

Winston shook his head and straightened up. "I stand corrected. Maybe I should get a pair."

Holly smirked sourly at his words. "You haven't the legs."

A sound similar to cracking ice came from inside the hangar and the siren failed with a strange warped squawk. It took a few minutes but then a cloud of black sparkling dust began to fill the space. The smoking edge of a sphere expanded and subsumed the walls. With a rumble, and a sound like a pile of falling leaves, the whole building collapsed. The dust cloud did not go past a sharply defined perimeter as if the Q-Staff had created a glass bubble.

But then corrosive tendrils skittered across the ground, etching the pavement. A large section of the walls on the neighboring warehouses vanished into smoke. Spiderweb cracks shot through the fibercrete towards the group of witnesses. Smoke erupted from them. Everyone ran further back. They were almost back to the Sierra Madre before they felt safe again.

"Underground utility lines. I suspect the fabricators need some extra elements outside of its original reach," Count LaBlanc guessed.

A strong breeze began to grow. Flowers and dangling moss were tugged toward the epicenter of the nanofabrication cloud like streamers and flags. Some bird-like creatures tried to flee but vanished into ash as they flew the wrong way. They watched on, mesmerized at the miraculous horror evolving before their eyes.

Five rapid blasts followed by a long one from the Sierra Madre's horn made everyone jump, hearts about exploding with the shock. It waited a few seconds and then repeated. Hands slapped over ringing ears. An automated emergency warning.

"What the purg was that?" Holly shouted, shoving a finger in an ear, massaging it.

"No… no no no!" Winston went white as a sheet.

"What?" Count LaBlanc shouted in consternation.

"It's the Black Void alarm!" Winston shouted over his own ringing ears. "All commercial vehicles have them!"

He looked at the Count in pale terror. "Sorry LaBlanc, but playtime is over. You have minutes to get clear of this moon. Hypermach if you can, because this part of the Dream is going away forever!"

"Your alarm must be detecting the Q staff. It's acting like a black void," the Count protested.

"Not a chance!" Winston rebuked the noble.

"There!" Billy Joe shouted and pointed an enlarged hand into the distance. A ripple in the Dream rose over the horizon, rapidly expanding in size and intensity. Its black cloud form consuming the sky as it grew. Around its indistinct, cancerous blot, purple lightning shot out for thousands of miles in giant webs, helping the Void grow.

"Billy Joe, what's the Sierra Madre saying? How much time we got?" Winston demanded.

"I can't tell because someone," Billy Joe gave Holly an angry look, "screwed up the security protocols a little when she took over command."

"How was I to know?" she whined, as the precise control of her own emotions slipped and the tint of genuine remorse came out.

"Can you-" Winston started to say.

"Already rebooting her systems and kicking her hack job out," Billy Joe cut him off.

"You're not done offloading yet!" the Count shouted.

"And it's never going to happen here!" Winston shouted back. "That..." he pointed toward the darkening sky, "is far too close and my past experience tells me we have very little time to get in our ships and vamoose!" Winston turned to go.

"You leave without finishing the offload and I'll shoot you," LaBlanc declared. Winston sighed and bowed his head in disappointment. He turned to see the Count's pistol pointed at him. Winston slapped the gun out of his hand before the nobleman could pull the trigger, then landed a solid right cross to the nobleman's jaw, sprawling him out on his back, his turban rolled on the ground.

"That's the third time on this job someone's pointed a gun at me. People keep it up and I might get to like it." He looked at Holly, her face was drawn, eyes locked onto the growing cataclysm. "You gonna shoot me for him?"

The tangle of expressions that went across her face was incomprehensible to Winston, but she did not reach for her guns.

"These are yours, Miss Holly," Billy Joe set down the two cases and flowed back into the Sierra Madre.

"Sergeant! Shoot them if they try to leave!" the Count ordered, but his soldiers had scattered back to their trucks in hopes of getting to their own airships and escaping the oncoming oblivion.

Winston looked around. Nobody was answering LaBlanc's orders and his own pistol was yards away.

"You want an offload here? No problem! I can get this cheis off my back in a few seconds. Don't want it anyway. Billy Joe!" Winston yelled. "Drop the port side doors and mark them as down."

"Rog that, Hoss." Billy Joe said and ran the gravitational subroutine.

"What? No! No!" the Count shrieked.

All ten containers vomited their remaining cargo with a scary crash. Men and machines fell out as the gravity went sideways. When Blaugarten's local field took over, they smashed and skidded on the fibercrete in jumbled piles.

"There! Y'er empty," Winston shouted, and started up the keel entry. "Do with it as you will, in the time you have left. Maybe I'll get lucky and the void will eat up all your behnging abominations!" With a contemptuous wave of his hand, he entered the Sierra Madre's airlock and shut the door.

A second too late, Holly pounded on the door as Winston closed the seals. He stared out the small window at her with dead marble eyes.

"Uh uh, honey. Your ticket's punched with me. Go hitch a ride with the Count," He said. A wicked sneer slowly stretched across his lips.

"You bastard!" she screamed. "He's too busy picking up his toys."

"Not my problem," Winston said, locking her out.

"Please," she begged. "I'll make it worth your while!"

"You really think I'm that stupid?" Winston looked at her incredulously.

"I give you my word," she begged.

"Payback's as big a bitch as you are," Winston said and walked away.

Faintly, he heard her frustrated scream. "Nahq!"

114..

Winston's hands shook so bad he couldn't re-fire the grav fans. He stopped, clenched his fists, gave a shaking roar and pounded the arm rests several times. Lightning webs pushed the growing Black Void even closer, filling the sky from the canopy. It seemed to pulse as if it was breathing, always expanding.

That was when he noticed… something.

The Black Void's lighting flashed out farther than it's intended radius, leaving growing smoke where it spread. Just like the Q Staff did. Was LaBlanc right? Could it be that a Black Void was an out of control nano-disassembler cloud?

That disassociated analysis made Winston's world swim. His mind drifted away in enthralled astonishment, seduced by that incredible suspicion. The lead weights of blaring alarms and flashing lights lashed on to his thoughts and dragged him back into the moment. Winston shook himself and regained his focus. He had no time to fixate on that.

"Bubby, get me positive buoy on those containers. Max power to the couplers. We are out of here!" He barked, forcing himself to focus.

With a quick tug, Winston's crash frame slammed down, and he strapped in. A few shaky taps on the controls and the grav fans fired up. He gripped the yoke and watched the buoyancy creep down to zero.

"Come on… come on…" he begged the readout.

"Zero buoy! Punch it!" Billy Joe yelled.

Power poured into the Sierra Madre's fans generating enough brute force to pull her train of containers into the sky. Blaugarten's gravity well made the inertia drag tough to overcome at first. They jerked and yanked the empty containers skyward. Coupler buffers slammed against each other as the strain nearly overwhelmed them. They snapped back jolting Winston and Billy Joe, but the buffer generators, like pairs of magnets, kept the string of containers from crushing themselves into accordions as they broke from the moon's field.

Winston was gently pushed deeper into his seat as acceleration began to outpace the tug's compensators. A bubble of worry grew in his mind that they would fail. Images of being crushed flat cavorted through his mind.

"This is going to be so close," Winston grunted, putting his caboose toward the Black Void's hungry reach.

As they broke local atmosphere the first grasping tendrils struck Blaugarten, carving it up and then crumbling it like a rock crusher into smoke and dust.

"We're hypersonic," Billy Joe yelled.

"Yip," Winston agreed through clenched teeth. The sensation of acceleration lessened as the Sierra Madre raced to her maximum speed, a ripping thunderclap chased her wake.

"No implosion yet," Billy Joe said, his eyes locked on the rear cameras.

"There won't be until the Void's done eating," Winston said. "Distance from Blaugarten?"

"Not far enough. Lightning tendrils are still gaining," Billy Joe's voice climbed an octave in fear.

Winston pushed the engines to the max, feeling the shudder through the floor as the Sierra Madre reached max speed. The hull gave brief flashes of fire off her nose as the thicker air and clouds burned from their passing through.

"We're pulling away!" Billy Joe gave a hearty sigh of relief.

A contrail of smoke highlighted their escape. Their heat shields were glowing red and slowly turning yellow with the acceleration. Using the weather map, Winston aimed for gusts of lighter atmospheric viscosity. With careful maneuvering, the Sierra Madre ducked between clouds and thick pockets of atmosphere. Behind them clouds and asteroids turned into smoke and ash.

"How big is this thing going to get?" Billy Joe asked.

"Mighty big." Winston's voice strained. His eyes flicked sporadic glances between the controls and the void in the rear cameras. Ahead lay a collection of small populated skylands. They were too close. He could see the specks of people fleeing in their personal fliers and every airship they could get off the ground.

"Full size! Full size! She stopped growing!" Billy Joe shouted.

Winston held his breath, the Sierra Madre's rattling flight was the only sound.

"It's collapsing," Billy Joe said. Winston looked at the camera. The Black Void boiled in place for a moment on the scanners, then it started to fall in on itself, drawn back by inexorable cosmic force.

Winston wanted to throw up. "Valerie..." he whispered.

There was a bright purple flash that washed out the sky. The canopy auto-polarized to black and the energy wave washed over them. Alarms wailed and a few touchscreens went blank. Their circuit breakers snapping open from the EMP wave washing them.

"We've ruptured a seal and backup coupler on containers number one and four! Telemetry link is cut after can number five! Computer is working to reestablish. All primary couplers still show green," Billy Joe said, relieved.

"Get those back up and fix that seal, Bubby, or we'll lose the whole string. We're still way too close!" Winston ordered. He watched the implosion wave chasing them, moving at megasonic speeds as air rushed to fill the hard vacuum left behind. Billy Joe flew from the engineering console, closed the inner cab door and slid to the container access hatch. He split his arms in twain and mounted tool orbs from the maintenance locker onto his two new pseudopods. He lashed himself on to the Sierra Madre's safety line and went out the exterior hatch.

Winston flipped through the exterior cameras to keep an eye on Billy Joe. The sound of the hypersonic air roared as the minute safety eddy was still terrifyingly strong. Little zephyrs bit chunks out of Billy Joe's arms like piranhas.

The second backup coupler on the container was flashing red warning lights on its control panel. Some debris must have hit it in the cavitation between the faring, or the flash might have caused an electrical surge. Billy Joe moved in slow motion, his utility skirt's strained to keep hold of the rails and lifelines that were taut to the point of breaking. Any biological life would have been torn apart instantly.

Slowly he stretched over and toggled the manual reset for the coupler. A larger crosswind tore nanites free from his utility arms almost losing one of his tool orbs to the Dream. Winston could see his partner being sandblasted away by bits of smoke and vapor that snuck into faring eddy. A few more adjustments to the controls and Billy Joe resealed the panel. Green across the board.

"Looks like a software glitch," he commed back.

Winston looked back at the camera from the rear container and swallowed hard.

"Then get back in here, the implosion wave is coming fast," Winston warned. The hazy edge of the wave, though slowing down would still reach them too soon.

With one final check, Billy Joe tested the container hatch lock and it slid open.

"Hoss! Container One's open! Latch's busted, internal gravity is offline." Billy Joe could see scraps of dunnage and dirt whirling like dervishes with the wind in the zero gee environment of the container.

"I don't give a behng! You have maybe 15 seconds and then anything not inside is gonna get sucked right off this ship! In or out Bubby!" Winston shouted.

Steeling himself, Billy Joe reached across and gave a 5 second spot weld to the container door then dragged himself back inside the Sierra Madre and closed the access hatch.

The implosion wave hit just as the hatch locked. It felt as if the ship's grav fans reversed flow in an emergency brake. Winston was thrown against his cushioned crash frame, hard. Without it, he would have slammed through the carbon scored nose of the canopy. Billy Joe had to grab onto the floor with every nanite in his skirt, turning it into a huge suction cup to keep him from doing the same.

Off to their eight o'clock the skylands began to slide past them, some breaking up from the pull, others colliding in horrifying explosions of rock.

Winston couldn't take his eyes off the rear monitor. The horrifying void mesmerized him for the second time in his life. The space was absolutely clear of everything that had existed mere minutes before. Everything in the implosion's radius was falling into its center.

The Sierra Madre shook as the winds grew and grew. Man and mech were slammed about by the turbulence despite inertial buffers. Winston lost track of time as he fought to maintain control. The skylands accelerated past them on their way to a new position in the Dream. It was possible that a new moon of compressed matter might be the result, some isolated amused part of his brain thought. A new Blaugarten was being created by the matter drawn into the growing gravity well of collecting mass.

A bright shimmering blob was approaching them with froth and spray.

"You have got to be cheising me!" Winston blurted out. "A waterberg?"

Winston turned to avoid the raging mountain-sized mass of free-floating water. As he turned hard to avoid a direct hit on the liquid mass, the hypersonic winds grabbed the Sierra Madre and began to try to tear the train apart. Coupler alarms screamed as they skimmed its surface, blasting through the foaming spray rising from its surface.

"Keep turning, Hoss!" Billy Joe shouted. "Use the wind's draw to slingshot us out!"

Winston ran with the Bubby's suggestion. "Just like a heavy moon, use its force..." he muttered, praying that the water shooting through the fans wouldn't burn them out. "... and achieve escape velocity."

The Sierra Madre burst out of the water, using the winds help to make for much smoother flying. Now instead of fighting full force against the Dream's atmosphere rushing to fill the void he was now at an angle to it, spiralling away. The route was longer but his power drain dropped by half. Winston wove up and down to avoid slow moving debris pulled in to where Blaugarten and a fair chunk of the Dream existed.

Winston sighed. "Good suggestion, Bubby. Really good. Looks like we'll make it after all."

"I guess we got a tug wash out of the bargain, too." Billy Joe said.

Winston laughed at the mundane side effect of their near disaster. Like an emergency relief valve engaged just before the boiler exploded. The high shrill hysterics left him with a hitch in his side and tears down his cheeks as the hysterics finally subsided.

Billy Joe stared at him blankly head cocked ever so slightly like a puppy. Winston felt light. He could see that his partner couldn't understand but now wasn't the time to explain either.

Now he was able to focus on more mundane needs of the Sierra Madre. With a few deft taps, he cleared out the list of comm warnings and standard mass casualty and disaster alerts. It looked like for the most part those who weren't digested by the Void escaped without too much trouble, and those left probably couldn't be helped.

Just as Winston started pulling up the charts to plot a lane back to Consolidated Freight with the containers the "All Comm" channel indicator lit up. Someone in this disaster was broadcasting in the clear for everyone to hear. Usually it was just some entertainment Dataoid who was tone deaf to tragedy or a news network reporting. Hard to believe they'd be here so quick though. Curious, Winston flipped the comms open to give a listen.

"Mayday, mayday, mayday," came the ancient cry for help. "This is Bonavitae Pharma Clinic calling for any vessel in the vicinity to evacuate our facility. A Black Void has imploded nearby and our skyland is falling into the collapse. There are four hundred patients and attendant staff. We need immediate evac. ETA to impact with the debris core is two hours. All our vehicles were destroyed by the event. Mayday, mayday, mayday! We need immediate evac to any and all vessels in the area." The voice broke off for a moment. "Please help us..." they whispered before breaking into hopeless sobbing and the transmitter went dark.

15..

"Bonavitae Clinic, this is the Sierra Madre, please respond," Winston said, his mouth dry and tasting of copper.

He repeated the call a half dozen more times with silence as his only reply. He turned in to the flow of the slowing winds aiming for the source of the transmission. Carefully, the Sierra Madre picked a safe passage through the skylands as they were drawn toward their inevitable doom at the implosion epicenter.

"Maybe something happened to their transmitter?" Billy Joe guessed.

"It's possible, but we're going in anyway to make sure. I'm going to get them out. Nobody else dies because I didn't go this time," Winston said.

"But what about H-" Billy Joe protested.

"LaBlanc isn't that stupid. He probably bolted shortly after we did, and took her with him." Winston rationalized.

"Maybe. Look, Hoss, Valerie and Emmy weren't your fault. Nobody coulda saved them," Billy Joe commiserated, touching the true root of Winston's reckless choice.

"I said nobody else!" Winston roared back, redoubling his focus on his flight path he'd chosen to reach the clinic.

"Okay, Hoss," Billy Joe soothed. "We'll do it your way."

Winston's white knuckled fists twisted around the yoke handles, trying to crush them between his fingers as the rage and confusion swirled in his heart. This time, nobody dies because of me, he repeated over and over like a mantra. One part prayer, one part flagellation of his soul.

The debris field became thicker the closer they got to the source of the distress call. Clouds of gravel and avalanches of mud and mangled plant life flew by like smoke in the wind. The Sierra Madre snaked through the tightening gaps, and Winston kept blasting out hailing comms broad spectrum, just in case they were on a different channel.

"Yeah. I think you're right, Bubby. Good chance their antennae was taken down by debris," Winston said softly.

"We pull this off and it's going to be a driver's room legend," Billy Joe said, a little prideful.

Winston ignored him, lost in his own mutters.

Finally, Winston tapped open the comms again. "Dunno if you can hear me Bonavitae Clinic, but I'm dragging ten empty cargo containers and we're fifteen minutes out. Telescope shows your skyland tumbling pretty bad, but looks like you still have local gravity. Get everyone you can to move fast ready at what looks like a central courtyard. I'm going to set down in a coil right in the middle. If you have any security or anti-airship defenses still working, shut 'em down. If something shoots at me, I will abort this rescue attempt. If you are receiving me, get a light or bonfire going in the middle of that courtyard... anything bright. I'll see it on your next rotation. Sierra Madre out."

Winston let out a long sigh. "Well, let's see what happens now."

The skyland rolled around once again. No light in the telescope. Just some faint movement of people running about. Then a second rotation with nothing.

"Maybe their receiver is down too?" Billy Joe suggested when there was no sign they had heard their transmission.

Winston slewed around an asteroid that arced across their intercept. "Could be, Bubby, but we're going in anyway."

The implosion winds had ended, but Newton's Laws of motion were still in full effect. Masses as big as skylands would take tens, if not hundreds of thousands of miles to stop from those speeds, but that was a luxury they would not receive. They were destined to become a part of the growing patchwork moon.

They entered final approach and timed their landing with the rotation, Winston saw that the implosion had scoured most of the surface of the skyland. Anything that wasn't bolted into the bedrock or strong enough to resist the winds was stripped clean off.

As Bonavitae's skyland rotated around again a hundred or more faint emergency chemlights stuck out from windows on all floors, ringing the courtyard.

"All right!" Winston shouted with joy, and Billy Joe let out an autotuned rebel yell. "Curl her up, Bubby! We're going in hot."

He flicked open the comms.

"We see you Bonavitae! Get clear and be ready, we're going to have containers open toward every side. You just get them in fast. We have no time to play. The debris is getting too thick and in five minutes, we're closing the doors and off we go," Winston said.

Then a thought came to him, and he flicked open the comm again. "If you need a quarantine container, use the last one. Let's not get us all killed a few weeks or months down the line by some contagion you guys have isolated."

The Sierra Madre contorted in the air like a falling cat, as the zero buoyancy containers whipped around and curled up into a ring before landing. The string of containers fit inside with only a few minor scrapes and blew out the few remaining clinic windows. Winston flipped on the PA system.

"Opening containers in five seconds," he announced as a wash of falling gravel shot through the top floor of the clinic like an autocannon.

The doors dropped all the way, and ramps extended.

"Go, go, go! Get inside and stay clear of the door once in!" Winston called over the PA.

Staffers opened the doomed clinic doors and patients poured out. Some were pushed on stretchers, others in tanks, but most were able to move on their own, shuffling like herded cattle entering the barn. Equipment of questionable and unidentifiable types followed.

"Take only what you must! Three minutes!" Winston shouted over the PA at a patient pushing a stretcher loaded up with a hoard of personal possessions. "You! You there! Drop the luggage. Only essentials!" An orderly rushed over to gather up the shrieking man, leaving his possessions behind.

Something metal hit on the other side of the building like an artillery shell. An incredible blast shook the skyland as it obliterated a wing of the clinic. The fountain of debris that vomited into the sky hung there till it was caught by the growing gravity well of the freshly forming planet in front of them, and slowly fell away. Winston watched his gauges as conflicting gravity sources made everything slide like it was on the surface of a stormy ocean, the skyland disintegrating beneath their feet as it rotated.

"Bubby, we got a pile up on a ramp," Winston noted as a crowd of people stopped before the first container, milling around confused. "Get back there and make sure nobody's getting stupid on us," Winston ordered.

"Rog dat, Hoss." Billy Joe went back, cut the spot weld and entered the first container. One person stood at the door, an X-Ray carbine aimed at the patients.

Holly.

"That's right! You step up here, you diseased meatbags, and I will end you before you can turn your head and cough!" She threatened. Behind her was a stack of crates that had somehow not fallen out of the containers when Billy Joe had dumped the cargo on Blaugarten.

"Miss Holly? How..?" Billy Joe blurted out, jaw dropped low. Then giving himself a shake he ordered, "Ahhh, we ain't got time! Get these people in there! We only got a few minutes left!

"You see the amount of cheis they're dragging?" she shouted, gesturing to the medical equipment. "There's no room!" Holly snapped back.

"Don't make me do something you'll regret, Miss Holly." Billy Joe warned.

"Are you threatening me, Bubby?" she sneered, using his nickname.

"Yes, Miss Holly, I am. Let them in or get out," he drawled.

"Well bless yo' li'l heart!" she mocked.

Billy Joe's face got hard with anger. Suddenly the container wall behind her on the inside of the coil dropped down and her world was twisted sideways as Billy Joe shifted the gravity field. She, and her squirreled away cargo, was thrown out while he remained suctioned to the container.

Dazed, Holly looked up from the pile of the weapons and crates she had managed to steal from LaBlanc in astonishment.

"I warned you," Billy Joe said as the door she was thrown through closed.

"What's going on? We're taking too long," Winston commed back to Billy Joe.

"Had to throw a tramp off our train," Billy Joe said. "Holly snuck on. She musta squirreled away a bunch of cargo just before we locked up and blasted off from Blaugarten. It's all off now. Evacuees are almost done boarding."

"Xiao on a cracker..." Winston breathed.

"Right?" Billy Joe asked. "What kind of blowback is she gonna cause us next?"

"Guess we'll find out once we get clear of all this," Winston commed back and closed the link.

The rest of the loading went surprisingly quick as the last of the patients, staff and even a few visitors were on-boarded.

Winston made the Sierra Madre buoyant while Billy Joe went through the containers securing their refugee's cargo. With a terrifying grinding moan the skyland began rubbing against an even larger chunk of planetoid and began shattering. Fissures opened up through the courtyard and split the clinic in two and the Sierra Madre floated away like a fly before a swatter. Carefully, Winston maneuvered through the tightening debris field as the skylands turned into clouds of boulders and dust. Winston breathed a sigh of relief as they cleared the disaster area unharmed.

Several hours of careful flying later, they worked their way out of the crisis zone and to safety once again. The sensors chirped new contacts and automatically swung the telescope to look at the source. A small task force of Xiao's warships decelerated from megasonic speeds.

"Got here a little too late, didn't 'cha?" Winston gloated, stabbing his finger at the images on the telescope monitor, then quickly put more debris in between the Sierra Madre and the Imperial forces, quietly slinking away. The imperial megajets arced off toward the newborn baby moon, confirming they were not pursuing the Sierra Madre.

"That's right! Yeah! We were never here, and there's no more evidence we did our job! Uhn!" His fist pounded his armrest in ecstatic relief.

"And now, let's just make sure you never notice," Winston whispered and made a slight course adjustment. The Sierra Madre and her string of containers descended into a cloud layer of dense bauxite dust and vanished in the interference. When the imperial signals fell off the scanners it was the first time in almost a week that Winston felt even a little safe.

The debris fields were now in their wake, and they popped into a clear band of the Dream where the winds were calm and the skies clear revealing the layers of the Dream. Technicolor billows formed a floor and ceiling as the Sierra Madre dove back toward known civilized sky. He wasn't sure how long it had been before he finally felt strong enough to stand, let alone talk to anyone. Winston set the autopilot for a leisurely slow course toward Consolidated's nearest container yard.

He popped his crash frame and stood up with a groan. A slow stretch released the pent up tension. He felt it ebb from his body with every roll of his shoulders. He went to fetch his bumblebee and readied to do an inspection of his new passengers and cargo.

"I suppose the polite thing to do would be to greet our passengers," Winston said to himself. "Not to mention see how Bubby's getting on."

16..

Winston went back to find chaos. Pained cries and moans of fear filled the container. Desperate nurses and orderlies worked with the patients to treat their wounds and calm them from the trauma of the event.

"I sure hope you're not contagious," Winston mumbled to himself, squinting disapprovingly at a patient on a gurney who twitched uncontrollably.

"Nurse? Nurse?" Winston called out to a felinoid woman dressed in a crisp white uniform with a few spots of blood. She looked up from checking the portable life support equipment and came over to Winston.

"Who are you? The pilot?" she asked.

"I am. Who's in charge?" Winston demanded.

"I..." she looked around the container, packed full of people in various states of trauma. "I didn't see Doctor O'Chaudry get on. He's our clinic administrator. He might be anywhere. So many people were hurt by falling debris, nobody's where they should be. Most of the people we managed to get on here were hurt in the rock storm.

"Nobody's contagious?" Winston asked.

"Contagious? No, sir. None of our patients are contagious," the cat lady reassured. "We isolated the dangerous patients in the last two containers like you requested. They're all confined so you won't be able to get in there without an armed guard."

"Why's that?" Winston asked.

"For your safety," she said matter-of-factly. "That's where we put Basement Three."

"What's so special with Basement Three and why do I need to be kept safe from what was in there if no one's contagious?" Winston said sharply.

Her cat eyes went wide and ears planed back in shock at his question. "Excuse me, but I must go," she muttered quickly.

"Whoa, whoa, whoa, lady!" Winston blurted, scruffing her as she turned.

"Let me go," She yowled, showing fangs.

"Not till you tell me what you meant. And if you scratch me, I'll lay you out," Winston threatened, balling up a fist.

She hissed in anger, unable to break his grip before giving in. The other staff watched, unsure of whether to get involved. Winston's threatening glare gave them pause.

"That's the secure ward where we keep the criminally insane. We're a psycho-pharmacology clinic. We do end studies for beneficial psychotropic drugs as well as conditioning therapy for those deemed too dangerous to the Imperium and other tribal governments and kingdoms."

The hair on Winston's neck and arms stood up.

"Everyone? As in every patient onboard? Is insane?" Winston asked in a subdued conspiratorial tone.

"Almost. Most aren't dangerous," the nurse said, then added more seriously, "Except for the ones from Basement Three. But they're sedated and restrained. Nothing to worry about."

"Now... if you'll excuse me," The nurse took the opportunity of Winston's shock to jerk free.

She walked backwards a few steps, growling, then turned to aid another injured patient.

"Cheis," Winston whispered.

He scanned the room. No one was panicking anymore or showing much emotion. The orderlies and nurses had regained control and were checking patient vitals. Despite the relative normalcy of what was an impromptu ER, it wasn't right. Winston bolted from the container back to the Sierra Madre, as if insanity was an airborne contagion. He leapt across the gap and sealed the door.

"Bubby? Bubby!" he commed. "Got your ears on mench? Bubby!" his voice cracked.

"I hear ya, Hoss," Billy Joe drawled back.

"Listen, I need you to find the doctor in charge back there. Goes by the name O'Chaudry. I have to keep my hands on the tiller. Bring him up and stay forward of container eight."

"Why?"

"Just do what you're told!" Winston slapped off the comm and put his head in his hands, his body trembling from stress due to the complications his passengers would probably cause.

When he looked up, a green comm notification from Mother pulsed. He tapped it open.

"Winston, I don't know what's been going on with you and Billy Joe, but congratulations. You are now financially secure for a while. The payment processed out just fine. When you're done offloading, return the containers to the Consolidated Freight yard in Terezad in the Rusi Archipelago. They will waive the container charges if you do that move for them. Please confirm ASAP, and we can talk in realtime once you are on site there. Mother out."

Winston frowned for so long his head hurt. He couldn't take these containers loaded up with crazy people... criminally crazy people into that xenophobic police state. He was stuck between his conscience and cash. If he brought them to Terezad he might be stuck in an uncomfortable spot for a long long time as they tried to sort out the nutters he just dropped on their doorstep. Of course, the late fees and any damage to the containers would be a painful sting if he went right back to home base in Pseudomaha. Tolerable, but painful. Plus he'd still have to explain himself. What the purg was he going to do?

A rapidly pulsing comm alert popped up. Mother, priority one. He tabbed it open.

"Winston! Comm me! I just heard there was a Black Void event in that zone. Are you okay?" Mother broke off for a moment in an Dataoid form of pacing and began muttering to herself. "Oh I'll never forgive myself. What have those idiots done now? Nothing was supposed to happen. Simple job. What went wr-" the transmission cut off.

So Mother had known where they were going, and possibly more. Winston hit record.

"Mother, Winston. We're fine but we have some complications. Unable to return containers to the requested location directly. Please relocate to a hub in this zone for real time comms." Winston provided an out of the way tugstop where they might talk privately. "We'll be there in eleven hours. Winston out."

"Hoss?" Billy Joe said through the intercom. "Door's locked. Care to open it up? I have someone who needs to talk to you," Billy Joe asked.

"Is it this O'Chaudry guy?" Winston asked.

"No."

"Are they sick?" Winston winced.

"What? No," Billy Joe said, mildly confused.

Winston unlocked the door and Billy Joe came in with a woman who gave a frightened whimper at crossing the gap between container and tug.

The two entered the cab.

Billy Joe guided a woman dressed in modest, neo-victorian mourning dress very refined black clothes that spoke of breeding and deep wealth. They were.

"Hello," the woman greeted him once she regained her composure and held out her hand. "I'm Doctor Amanda Junker." She was older than him, but not elderly.

"How do, Doctor Yoonkur?" Winston pronounced the unfamiliar sounding name carefully. "Are you in charge?"

"No. I am... or rather was, a visitor at the Bonavitae clinic. Here to see my brother-in-law," she explained holding up a visitor's badge.

Winston looked a question at Billy Joe who shrugged in return.

"Don't blame him, sir," she said politely, "I intercepted him and asked him to bring me to you before you met Dr. O'Chaudry. You may not know, Bonavitae Pharmaceuticals is not what it seems."

"Ma'am, I already know it was an asylum of sorts. Worse, I think they might still be doing some very bad things," Winston hazarded.

The doctor sighed, nodding. "There are patients here that ought not be, and that's why I came to talk to you."

"Your brother-in-law is here against his will?" Winston asked delicately.

"Yes. He's an archaeologist, and a few of his discoveries angered some of Xiao's courtiers and they had him committed. 'For his own good', of course, and to protect society from his crazy ideas." She gave a small laugh. "As if knowing the past was a crazy idea."

"From your tone, I assume you were trying to free him?" Winston said.

"I was," Doctor Junker admitted without hesitation. Almost strident in the proclamation.

"Does your husband approve of your efforts?"

"Yes, he approves," she said then paused, clenching her jaw a few times. "Or rather, he did approve... is the more accurate statement. I'm a widow."

Winston was caught short at what to say. "I'm sorry for your loss?" he stammered.

"Sixty one months we tried. Then after his passing I alone strove to get Quentin out of the hands of these brain butchers."

"Now don't tell me that your husband died under mysterious circumstances digging into evidence to rescue his brother?" Winston said, giving a disbelieving sidelong glance and smirk.

"It would make a good novel if that were the case, wouldn't it?" she laughed grimly. "But, no. He died of natural causes. But for the sake of Quentin I used a small portion of my late husband's fortune to provide for him in this place. Bribes to keep him safe and his mind undamaged by what they call therapy. It let him have a few luxuries that kept him grounded. As if books and art could be called luxuries."

"So your brother-in-law is a little..." Winston spun a finger around his ear with a cuckoo whistle.

She didn't react to his callous implication.

"You would have a hard time keeping your sanity if you were locked up, gaslit by the staff and medicated like a schizophrenic," her voice was colorless. "I keep the worst away from him. Thankfully that bastard, O'Chaudry, is a corrupt one. Bonavitae was Quentin's oubliette and I was the only person left who kept his memory alive. He's a cipher to the Dream now. His enemies have purged all his data from the cloud network and disassociated or scrambled what remained till truth and lies became indistinguishable. His accomplishments on record have been re-attributed to others academics and intellectuals. In this manner, poor Quentin has been effectively written out of existence and would have died of neglect long ago if not for me maintaining my vigil."

Winston had a distinct image of the good doctor standing on a widow's walk of a large weather-beaten house on the edge of a skyland, looking out over a vast empty sky, candles burning in the windows below.

"What would you propose I do?" he asked.

"Let us off somewhere. Anywhere I can hire transportation, or something else to get us home," Doctor Junker pleaded.

"If he's a patient, I think the guards would mind, don't you?" Winston pointed out

"This may very well be his last chance. The local patient records did not make it off the skyland and are surely destroyed, The data link went down when the black void imploded so nothing was sent, and he is already a ghost in the data clouds," she wrung her elegant black clutch purse in her gloved hands. "If he is reintegrated into some kingdom's or tribe's surveillance system, they will re-commit him and I don't know how I will track him down again. I'm certain he will vanish, this time for good."

Winston looked at her, unsure if she was telling the truth or some sort of sociopath spinning a tale.

"What happens if I say no?" Winston tested.

"I would offer to pay you," she countered.

"What if I asked an unreasonable sum? Would you offer something else?" Winston said cautiously.

Doctor Junker searched his eyes. She caught his meaning but it was clear she was unsure if he meant it.

"I… suppose I would look for another way to free him," she said quietly, her mouth tight, brow furrowed.

Winston gave a loud snort and shook his head. "Good. You have limits and a sense of self worth. Okay, doctor, If it's possible to free your brother-in-law, we'll work something out, but no promises."

She blinked, her mouth opened just a sliver, the words caught inside.

As if to make sure no one forgot about her, the Sierra Madre gave a series of beeps to alert Winston and Billy Joe of a mandatory maintenance warning to one of her inertia compensators.

"Listen," Winston leveled with her. "I'm screwed with this situation already. These containers you're riding in? They have to go to Terezad. The type of place that would quietly black bag us and we'd wake up... if we ever woke up... in a slave labor camp someplace horrid a few days later. I need to dump everyone somewhere where they won't bat an eye at a train load of well-medicated crazy patients accompanied by armed orderlies, nurses and doctors. Now if you can tell me where tha-"

"Nova Tortuga," she said, not letting him finish.

"You... what?" Winston was shocked to hear such a lady mention that nigh mythical skyland.

"Nova Tortuga. I'm familiar with the place. They have a rather laissez-faire attitude toward this sort of immigration," Doctor Junker said firmly.

"That's because nobody sane wants to go there, and those that do are dangerous as behng! It's as rowdy to this day as it was eons ago when water touched her shores instead of sky."

"It seems that the Commodore's press agent is earning his pay if you believe that," the Doctor said, with a little shake of her head and thin smile.

"What?" Winston was confused.

"All the Commodore's propaganda about Nova Tortuga seems to be having the proper effect on people like you," Doctor Junker said with a strong hint of knowing far more.

"Who?" Winston tried to close the gap in his understanding.

"So, are you saying that you won't go there?" Doctor Junker asked pointedly.

"I'm not saying anything for another 12 hours. Then I'll have my bearings and decide how to go forward. Till then, go back and stick with your brother-in-law and I'll send Billy Joe back when the time is right."

The Doctor gave a sharp nod of agreement "Thank you, Mr...?"

"You can call me Winston," he said.

"Thank you, Winston. You're doing the right thing," she said.

Winston motioned to Billy Joe to take her back. A moment later, he was alone in the cab.

"You say I'm doing the right thing, Doctor, but I don't know if that's true or I'm now just one of the inmates," he griped to himself.

All the stress seemed to settle in Winston's bones. With a groan he got up and decided it was time to take a rest and recharge.

He sent a text to Bubby.

SIERRAMADRETUG: "Bubby, I'm going to hit the rack for a few. Lock the door when you come back up after you're done,"

He moaned and shuffled toward his sleeper

SMLOADMASTER: "You got it, Hoss. Things are looking fine. Try to get some real sleep if you can,"

Billy Joe sent back.

Winston let out a weak laugh.

SIERRAMADRETUG: "After what we just went through? Purg no! I'll be lucky if my nightmares don't leak into the instance. Nite."

He stepped inside the sleeper and closed the door behind him.

The smell of sex hit his nose like a fist. Lust overpowered his thoughts and his body no longer obeyed his control. He spun to look for the source, whipped open the shower door and found Holly standing there.

"Two things, flyboy," she growled, limbic manipulator at full blast, "Firstly, you and your lumper tried to leave me for dead. Twice, and I'm not happy about it."

The tsunami of lust overwhelmed all his rational thoughts, smashing them and leaving his primitive lizard brain in charge which lurked at the root of all men's minds. Winston lunged at her with a rutting bellow.

Holly's foot flashed out, kicking him in the chest. Winston left the floor and flew the two yards away into the wall over his bed. Bonelessly, he fell down half on and off the bed, face smacking the dirty floor.

~~~

"And secondly," she gloated haughtily over his unconscious body, "You still have no idea who you're dealing with."

Holly picked up his body like he was a stuffed animal and crammed him into the bunk. She threw the blanket over him, slipped his simulation rig on his head and turned it on. Wedging herself between him and the wall, she all but vanished from sight. As she settled in, she fired up her
~~~

internal linkup, and discovered Billy Joe forgot to change the passwords. She chuckled to herself, accessed the autopilot and uploaded new coordinates.

"Kinky dreams, flyboy. It's been a long and cheisy day," she whispered, limbic manipulator still on full blast, rattling his subconscious like a mis-calibrated gyroscope, then she drifted off to sleep.

INTERLUDE –
XIAO SEES ALL

Xiao gazed out from the palace harem's large veranda at a mountain range he made. It was one of tens of thousands of palaces he kept scattered throughout his Dream. All unique, designed to reflect a different mood or nuance. This palace he named "Romantic Astonishment". And it was. The winds sighed musically across the moon through trees with hollow branches, creating melodic chords with one another.

His lust recently slaked, he lazily contemplated the myriad of things that required his attention. With a thought, he issued orders and projected his will through his wired connections. With a mere whim, a kingdom of millions of his subjects could prosper or fall.

A humanoid came out on the veranda as Xiao enjoyed the view and the music of the twilight that passed for night in his domain. He was tall, impossibly slender, dressed in a long droopy robe of deep blue. The Imperial eye on his chest was bisected by the opening of his robe like the pages of a book laid open to read. He glided soundlessly to stand behind his emperor and bowed before speaking.

"The Eye of Xiao sees all," the being said in prayerful reverence. In front of his face he pressed his palms together, fingers spread with thumbs pointing straight up and down in the imperial salute, "Hail Xiao."

The Emperor did not turn to address his soft-footed servant. "Narrator, what have you for me?"

"A hero in the making, your imperial majesty," the Narrator's voice quivered with excitement.

Xiao's eyebrows rose a little.

"A hero you say?" Xiao said with a faint smile.

"One who would greatly benefit from your mellifluous nature, oh Mighty One," the Narrator said with barely restrained joy. "A man with the qualities you desire in a hero. Possibly a hero for your people. A sentient able to unite them in revolt against you. If properly cultivated he might provide a true challenge." The Narrator's voice trembled in bliss.

"This is pleasing news," Xiao said and turned to face his servant, enjoying the man's ecstatic state.

"Oh yes, your eminence," the Narrator sighed.

"Then come!" Xiao said, "Sit by my fire and tell me the story of my new hero, and I will contemplate his future."

The two sat down across from each other over a low firepit that gave off a warm hypnotic flicker and the Imperial Narrator began to tell Xiao the tale.

"Once again, my Lord, another hero is distinguishing himself from among the faceless billions of your subjects. Your prophets foretell the great deeds and tragedies he is about to endure…"

~   ~   ~

"Lucid Reality"

PREVIEW

Billy Joe busied himself with minor repairs on the containers' exteriors for the last few hours as the Sierra Madre coasted along at a dead slow pace.

He had given up doing repairs inside. It was almost impossible to get anything done with all the refugees. They were always underfoot and the staff kept getting in his way with questions. One patient desperately tried to eat his utility liquid skirt because the patient claimed it looked like "smoked maple syrup with sugar crystals".

An educated guess suggested the refugees had enough water, emergency rations and medical supplies to last them a day or two, but Billy Joe sure hoped they could offload these people before things got ugly. Bionts got dangerous when deprived of the essentials of life and comfort.

Then there was the constant flood of questions from passengers that he had no answer for.

Yes, we were safe.

Yes, we would disembark soon. Don't touch that!

No, I don't know what time dinner is.

How should I know if that was infected? See a nurse.

No, I don't want to play holocards.

Stop grabbing my nanosand, I don't grab your hair!

Billy Joe gave a little shudder with that last thought. He ground smooth the last remnants of his spot weld on the container. Now the lock worked properly. Satisfied, he went forward to the cab. The airlock closed behind him, making the sigh he wished he could make.

While putting his tools away, he heard the nav computer bleeping they were an hour out of their destination. Next to it, the comm suite showed Mother sent a note. He tapped to open and saw she was in livecomm range. Good enough for him.

Winston must have gotten eight hours sleep according to Billy Joe's internal clock. The indu slid up to the sleeper door and gave it a good rap.

"Yo, Hoss!" he yelled. "Time to get yo'self up!"

No answer came.

"Hoss!" he shouted again. This time he banged the door a lot harder.

He heard movement but again, no answer.

"Come on, son, Mother's on the horn and she wants ta talk."

Billy Joe hoped Winston had not locked himself in his Levitown instance again. Switching to his own virtual interface, he dove into the Sierra Madre's server and called up Winston's private node.

Billy Joe attempted to dive in. An error rebuffed him, refusing access. Did it shut itself down? After a long lag, his second login attempt was accepted. He did a quick diagnostic of the simulation. The bio-rhythmic data report looked frozen but the program had not crashed. It was locked up at the loading montage, like it failed at start. Winston would have rebooted his software within seconds for it would have kicked him out as a safety feature. A power flux might have done it but they hadn't suffered any disruptions.

Billy Joe opened the only file he could, the error log. The same message ran every second for tens of thousands of seconds.

```
ERROR: #1279374.34VIT
<!Simulation could not connect!>
<Reason: Medical obstruction to neural
relays>
<Reason: Transmitters misaligned/out of
safe tolerance parameters>
<!*SYNAPSE BURN DETECTED*!>
<!*SEEK IMMEDIATE MEDICAL ASSISTANCE*!>
```

End of Preview

ACKNOWLEDGMENTS & THANKS

I would like to acknowledge the contributions of the following people:

Editor
Jane Lambert

Alpha Readers
Torfinn Brokke, Francois Henning,
Ben & Shannon Stepanek

Beta Readers
John Baldez, Steven Blevins, Emily Cruze, Lacy Loudon, Sean
McDaniel, J. Phillip, Ken Porter, Jessi Roberts, Caleb Smay,
Mike Tabor

Special thank yous to:
The Wordmenders Critique Group: Stephanie Dooley, K.T.
Sweet, Nathan Veyon, Jenn Lees, & Phillip Wilder.
Dave Lawrence for supplemental editing & criticism.
Laura Van Arandonk-Baugh for her generosity & mentoring

Thank you all!